Lutesong and Lament

Tamil Writing from Sri Lanka

Edited by Chelva Kanaganayakam

We acknowledge the support of the Canada Council for the Arts for
our publishing program. We also acknowledge support from the
Ontario Arts Council.

Cover photograph: section from *Vidivu*; photographer, Amaradas

National Library of Canada Cataloguing in Publication Data

Main entry under title:

  Lutesong and lament : Tamil writing from Sri Lanka

ISBN 0-920661-97-1

I. Tamil fiction–20th century–Translations in English.
2. Tamil poetry–20th century–Translations in English.
3. Sri Lanka–Politics and government–1978- –Fiction.
4. Sri Lanka–Politics and government–1978- –Poetry.
5. Tamil (Indic people)–Fiction. 6. Tamil (Indic people)–
Poetry. I. Kanaganayakam, C. (Chelvanayakam), 1952-

PL4758.55.E5L87 2001   894'.8117208   C2001-903764-3

Printed in Canada by Coach House Printing.

TSAR Publications
P. O. Box 6996, Station A
Toronto, Ontario M5W 1X7
Canada

www.candesign.com/tsarbooks

To R Pathmanabha Iyer

Whose passionate commitment to
Tamil literature
has inspired and sustained many of us

Contents

Introduction

CHELVA KANAGANAYAKAM

The anthology begins and ends with two poems that bear the same title and offer two different readings of the same myth. Almost five decades separate the two "Ahalikai" poems—the first written by
Mahakavi and the second written by Sivasegaram. The latter's decision to work with the same myth implies continuity, intertextual af-
filiation, and a consciousness about influence and complementarity.
Both poets share an awareness about the value and significance of
myth, of the role the sacred plays within the Tamil social and cultural
ethos. Despite its conventional metrical patterns and idyllic tone,
Mahakavi's reading marks a point of departure from traditional ac-
counts that valorize the role of the renouncer, celebrate the magna-
nimity of the god Rama, and implicitly critique the destructive power
of passion. Mahakavi shifts the reader's attention to the psychologi-
cal, finds reason to understand human passion, and asserts the value
of individual choice, even if the consequences of violating a moral
code may well be disastrous. For Sivasegaram the issue is one of
agency, of the denial of any subjectivity to the woman and of the par-
adox of seeking salvation in a god who has been oppressively patriarchal. There is a deliberate literalness about the poem that insists on
shifting the perspective from the sacred to the secular, from the male
to the female and from the allegorical to the particular. The role of
Rama, which is incidental to the first poem, becomes crucial to the
second.

Beyond the theme, the differences in tone and style are striking.
Mahakavi's aestheticism expresses itself in a style that is overtly lyrical and conventional in its use of stanzaic patterns and alliterations,
although the diction is kept within the frame of the spoken idiom.
The lyricism often lulls the reader into an acceptance of the kind of

artifice that the author is known for. Even in translation the mellifluity of Mahakavi is difficult to miss. Sivasegaram's poem is more startling in its repetitions, its gradual building up of emotion until the conclusion becomes a revelation of a very different kind. The spoken voice dominates without losing its sense of poetry, and if the lyricism is less ostentatious, the poem is, nonetheless, no less effective. The mixture of tones that characterize the poem becomes a measure of the conflicting impulses that underline the poem and give it a rich complexity.

It would be convenient to speak of these poets as constituting a beginning and an end, as two ends of a literary spectrum, but that would hardly be accurate. What they point to is a trajectory, a way of understanding a tradition of writing. Mahakavi started in the 1940s and wrote for three decades, during which he shaped contemporary literature in ways that make his work a watershed. He himself inherited a tradition of literature that began several centuries ago and includes poetry, prose and a considerable body of oral literature. The presence of a long tradition of writing that goes back almost twenty centuries and finds inclusion even in the Sangam poetry of South India has been an enabling aspect of Tamil writing in Sri Lanka. The distinctiveness of the literary tradition in Sri Lanka has been dealt with often enough by scholars, and suffice it to mention that the various influences that shaped this literature, including the period of colonial rule and the textuality of missionary activity, are important ones that led up to the contemporary period that begins in the 1940s. Religion, literature, and convention intersected to produce much of the literature that preceded the latter half of the twentieth century. To this day, that tradition continues in both written and oral forms, appealing to a broad spectrum of society at one level and to the informed at another. The present anthology begins with the contemporary period, not because the previous is less important, but because the more traditional writing requires a separate project altogether.

In retrospect, the work of the early poets who began in the 1940s and 1950s may appear to be removed from active social engagement, but they too cannot be dissociated from the political and cultural context of the time. The 1940s was, of course, a transitional moment, and as the country moved towards independence various identities were being shaped and reinforced in significant ways. Decolonization in Sri Lanka did not involve the kind of strident resistance that characterized other parts of the Commonwealth. And hence the absence of literature that actively fuelled nationalistic fervor and denounced the colonizers. But there was a growing sense of national and ethnic identity, with the two establishing an ambivalent relation to each other. Ethnic identity was in itself hardly homogenous, as distinct differences were apparent among groups that lived in various regions and claimed very different cultural traditions.

For the early poets of the contemporary period, including Mahakavi, Nilaavanan and Murugaiyan, the main task was to create a literature that signaled a shift to the demotic. While the oral tradition was always a rich presence, the two streams, the oral and the literary, occupied very distinct spaces with very little by way of interaction. These poets achieved a fusion of the two by bringing to a diverse readership a body of writing that insisted on its artifice while exploiting the rhythms of ordinary speech. The formal was thus made to look natural and the sacred was accommodated within the secular. Among the early writers Murugaiyan, as has often been noted, leans towards a kind of intellectual rigor while Mahakavi foregrounds the subjective and lyrical. In a larger sense their impulses remain similar in that they saw poetry as having a populist dimension while being resistant to the idea of completely jettisoning conventional forms. In the introduction to *Pathinoru Eelathuk Kavignarkal* (1984), MA Nuhman points out that the early writers were vocal in their opposition to free or unstructured verse. They recognized the need for literature to liberate itself from archaic metrical norms and stanzaic patterns, but they also demonstrated a healthy skepticism towards a random association of words that masqueraded as art. Nonetheless, helped no doubt by newspapers and journals that actively promoted local writing and by critics and academics who endorsed the legitimacy of local literature, these writers flourished.

In prose, short fiction became the leading form, facilitated to some extent by the conditions of publication. Novels did appear, but they were, and have been, smaller in comparison to the large number of short stories that have appeared either in individual collections or anthologies. For fiction writers, the models were already present, partly in the short fiction from the West, a necessary aspect of the school curriculum, and in the short fiction of South India. The main contribution of these early writers was to make the everyday available in a milieu that privileged the sacred and the esoteric. "The Silver Anklet" by Ilangayarkone is implicitly intertextual in that its form is conditioned by paradigms that are common in Western fiction. The story is about the sacred—in fact the narrative is a kind of pilgrimage, not unlike a quest narrative. The intervention here is the secular or the profane as material concerns shift the attention away from the religious. Material aspirations are not seen as antithetical to but as complementary to religious ones, and the human as against the religious takes centre stage as the story progresses. Landscape and space become crucial aspects of human life, and animals and ghosts are seen not as extraneous but as central to human life and relationships. The shifts in tone reveal the struggle of the author to include new perceptions, new ways in which a changing ontology gets reflected in art.

Ilangayarkone was neither the first nor the only one to shape new trends in fiction. Anthologies such as *Velli Pathasaram* bring together the diversity and richness of the early writers. As in poetry, one is struck by the heterogeneity, by the different impulses that seem to be at work in the writing. While the dominant mode appears to be a kind of critical realism, the differences among them are striking. Given the rich tapestry of divisions—social, religious and regional—the stories reflect very different perceptions of society, landscape and even the gods. For the writers of the fifties and the sixties, the driving ideology was Marxism, resulting in a body of literature that was sharply conscious of social inequalities, the hegemony of an oppressive caste system, the denigration of women, and so forth. K Sivathamby, who sees this phase as a major turning point, claims that it was this "trend of opposition to social oppression and deprivation, led by the Progressive Writers' Association, that created an unprecedented literary impact" (97). Interestingly, the concern with the marginalized also empowered writers such as Dominic Jeeva, whose works gave voice to a segment of society that had hitherto remained suppressed. Draw-

ing a useful comparison, Sivathamby rightly points out that "Tamil
Nadu had to wait till the 1990s for Dalits to write about themselves.
In fact, K Daniel, the eminent novelist who wrote *Panjamar*, is considered the forerunner of Dalit writing" (97). The large number of
writers who responded passionately to the multiple social forces of
these years paved the way for the startling changes of the next generation of authors.

Between these early writers and the burgeoning of diasporic writing in the last decade, lies a rich body of material that needs critical attention and explication and merits translation. Some of these are
available only in private collections, and the vagaries of publication
and distribution have prevented any systematic bringing together of
all the diverse and rich material. Occasional anthologies and limited
translations in special issues of journals in the West have tried to provide some sense of unity to this body of material. The present anthology, too, is a way of collecting and preserving an eclectic body of
literature.

Even a project such as the present one raises the issue of taxonomy,
of a scheme that would provide, if not a teleology, at least a system for
understanding and discriminating among a heterogeneous body of
material. Scholars, critics and essayists including K Kailasapathy, K
Sivathamby, M A Nuhman, M Ponnambalam, S Sivasegaram, A J
Canagaratna, Suresh Canagarajah and Cheran, to name a few, have in
fact suggested insightful ways of classifying this body of material.
Nuhman's introduction to a collection of poems by eleven poets ad-
vances a linear model. He is at pains to make comparisons and his
contention is that Tamil writing in Sri Lanka, unlike its counterpart in
South India that is either too solipsistic or given to obscurity, expresses itself with a sense of its social role. Having acknowledged the
limitations of his endeavour, he goes on to identify five generations
of poets, each of whom spoke with a different voice inspired by the
changing social and political conditions of the time. The argument is a
valid one and the changes he alludes to, from social concerns to political ones, from convention to spontaneity, from local to regional, for instance, do in fact appear in the poetry. Nuhman's central argument is
that while the writers in Tamil Nadu were polarized on the question of

individualism versus social commitment, the writers in Sri Lanka were able to achieve both.

Sivathamby's model, which emerges in his substantial body of critical material, stresses the societal as he maps a trajectory from a kind of universalism or solidarity along Marxist lines to political separatism along ideological lines. He sees the identity of the Tamil people as undergoing dramatic transformation in the last fifty years, with each phase finding expression in literature. His argument takes into account the diverse impulses generated by social, religious, and spatial considerations, but ties them together in a holistic reading of contemporary Tamil writing. Equally interesting is the thesis advanced by Suresh Canagarajah, who, in an essay that deals with poetry, frames a large body of literature within the boundaries of orality and orature. In the final analysis he too reinforces the notion that contemporary poetry dispenses with the overtly "literary" for a mode that works with forms of naturalness. In some respects Canagarajah provides the evidence to substantiate the claims made by Nuhman and Cheran in their introductions to *Pathinoru Eelathuk Kavignarkal* and *Maranothul Valvom* (1985) where they repeatedly drive home the gradual introduction of the spoken idiom into a mode that had been trapped in archaic conventions. Canagrajah's discussion of poems by poets such as M Ponnambalam, Shanmugam Sivalingam and Cheran reflects innovations in tone and diction that enabled orature to become the characteristic mode of Tamil poetry. All these are ways of talking about a varied corpus of literature whose thematic preoccupations and formal experiments require much greater exegesis than is possible in this introduction.

Among other things, all these models stress the remarkable heterogeneity in Tamil writing from Sri Lanka. Overshadowed by the literature from South India, and more recently by postcolonial preoccupations with writing in English, critics do not often recognize that multiple streams coexist and converge in Sri Lankan Tamil writing. Any taxonomy should recognize the many differences that distinguish writing in Jaffna from that in the East or the hill country. Even within the writing of one region, class, caste and religious affiliations, not to mention changes in landscape, account for major differences. To juxtapose a story by Dominic Jeeva with that of N S M Ramaiah or to read a poem by Cheran with that of Shanmugam Sivalingam is to be aware of remarkable ontological differences. These works bring the reader back to the issue of multiple identities, and the curious ways in which they retain their separateness despite circumstances that bring them together. Jayapalan and Nuhman may speak of similar subjects, but they do so in ways that suggest distinctions are as important as similarities.

The similarities become evident in the anthologies—some of the more important ones being *Velli Pathasaram, Pathinoru Kavignarkal* and *Maranothul Valvom,*which imply three different moments in Tamilian consciousness. All three have to do with shaping and recuperating identity. The first has to do with forms of consolidation. That is not to say that the literature did not reflect the deeply divisive forces within society. Caste, class, and gender, for instance, provided much of the conflict within the stories. In the story by NK Ragunathan, for instance, the injustices of caste surface, as in many stories and poems not included here. But whether it is such stories and poems that are fundamentally tendentious or those, such as the story by S Ponnuthurai, that work with reconciliation, the sense of collective identity is never in jeopardy. And that is in keeping with the times which, despite all its concerns, provided a sense of national belonging. The second phase, again coinciding with political events that polarized the ethnic groups, reveal a much greater consciousness about ethnic identity, about the need to articulate one's place within the nation.

The present collection of translations works with a thematic paradigm rather than a chronological or spatial one. Admittedly, such a scheme has its drawbacks, and it certainly raises several theoretical questions. But the rationale is that a dominant stream in Tamil writing juxtaposes active social engagement with a worldview that is holistic. Regardless of the vicissitudes of time, that impulse has remained, as is evident in works so dissimilar as the story by N S M Ramaiah, the poem "Gently Flows the River" by V I S Jayapalan and the story by S Ponnuthurai. Space and time separate these works, and if some are the result of observations and others of memory, they are central to a worldview. Ramaiah's story recalls the economic hardship of life in the hill country and its human cost, while Ponnuthurai's story moves at a leisurely pace, incorporating multiple points of view, masking the deep animosities and concerns of an extended family. Framing such stories is Jayapalan's poem, romantic and idyllic, suggesting that the river continues to flow, "obliterating hurt" (to use Derek Walcott's admirable phrase).

The next phase, which in many ways is also a crucial one, begins with the confluence of ethnic identity with nationalist dreams. While generalizations about this phase are likely to be problematic, it is important to recognize that initially this phase came into being with the political turmoil of the late 1970s and the early 1980s. The anthology entitled *Maranothul Valvom* brings together an imagination that had to confront realities that it had never known before. Even the more conventional writers appear to have felt the huge hiatus between the social criticism of the past and the trauma of the present. Cheran's introduction to the anthology he edited reveals the abrupt wrenching away from a world that, with all its limitations, made sense. Now it was chaos, cruelty and displacement on a scale that was unimaginable. Sivathamby mentions that this corpus is "unparalleled in terms of the experience it has recorded and the genuineness and sincerity with which it has been produced" (99). Inevitably, some of this poetry is tendentious, driven by the desire to espouse a particular stance. Others depict a revelatory quality, a sudden awareness of connections, across regions, caste, and class, an intensity that accompanies dispersal and fragmentation. On the one hand poetry assumes the quality of song as it appeals to the masses; on the other, it absorbs and works with a profusion of imagery that accessed an apocalyptic vision.

For the first time—this again has been pointed out by Cheran in his introduction and by several other critics—writing by women has become a constitutive aspect of Tamil writing. Issues of gender have always preoccupied writers, but as far as men wrote about women agency remained in the hands of men. Apart from a few notable exceptions, women hardly ever wrote more than occasional pieces. Now several women—some of them directly involved with the political struggle, and others displaced in the diaspora—have begun to write both poetry and short stories.

In a remarkably insightful introduction to Sivaramani's poetry, published five years after the death of the author in 1991, Chitralega Maunaguru, herself a poet of considerable stature, contextualizes not only Sivaramani's work, but also that of other women who broke free from the stereotypes that denied them any real agency. As essentialist formulations were actively resisted and cast away, women wrote with much greater confidence. The appearance of *Sollatha Sethigal* in 1985 suggested a shift as new voices emerged to claim a space for themselves. Avvai, Aazhiyaal and Zulfiqa Ismail, in addition to those who find inclusion in the present anthology, were now very much a part of the literary establishment.

In more recent years, women writers have produced literature from Europe, from Canada and from Australia. Displacement, as Salman Rushdie has eloquently pointed out in his essays, entails loss, but it also signals gain. No longer framed by patriarchy in quite the same way, women writers have produced exciting new literature, concerned with the complexities of human relationships. Nirupa, Uma, Ranjini, Thayanithy, Banubharathy, Ranji, Pratheebha, Tanya, Thurga and Sumathy Rooban, for instance, have shaped the course of contemporary writing in significant ways.

Alongside these new changes, several other poets were giving expression to the new realities brought about by an increasingly hostile political scene. In a short but powerful poem, Jesurasa encapsulates the uncertainty and violence of the two decades, beginning in the 1970s. The predictability of a previous era has now given way to the arbitrariness of violence. Cheran's poems, poignant and evocative, reach across ethnic divisions to remind the reader of a common humanity, while poets such as Solaikkili and Sivasegeram work with a profusion of images, sometimes startling in their apocalyptic intensity, to record the emotional trauma of violence.

The most recent phase of the literature grows out of and draws on the political turmoil but moves in new directions as a consequence of the diaspora. Written partly by displaced authors who, from Europe, North America or Australia, write about old or new homes, this literature fuses nostalgia with the cultural context of new lands. Paradoxically diaspora, combined with globalization, has prompted writers to forge new connections, experiment with new forms, and publish their works in both South India and Sri Lanka. The diasporic space, as anthropologists such as Dipanker Gupta have shown, is a particularly important one, incorporating sites that are remembered in ways that enable an empowering transformation.

"A Night in Frankfurt" is directly about displacement. "Visa" by Muttulingam might well be less representative of the predicament of exile, but it too drives home the notion that exile is much more than physical displacement. Hybridity manifests itself in complex ways, as writers struggle to merge two worlds, reflecting on the present and depicting the past through the prism of an alien culture.

Disapora is as much internal as it is external, as the story "The Gap" so poignantly demonstrates. As the symbiotic relationship between culture and landscape comes under stress, human relations suffer, and often the victims are the elderly, the marginalized, and the weak. In a culture that has been for the most part patriarchal, women have out of necessity assumed new roles and have felt the need to express multiple subjectivities, as is evident in some of their poetry.

The movement from one to another, all within a space of five decades, has given to writing in Tamil a range of material, depth of experience and a technical sophistication that makes it worthy of serious study. At a time when "nativist" critics and scholars have successfully argued for the need to pay closer attention to the contribution of vernacular literatures, there is an urgent need to make Tamil writing from Sri Lanka accessible to a wide readership through translation.

It is almost a cliché to state that literature is what is left out in translation. To some extent one laments what is lost in the translations that appear in this anthology. Sri Lankan Tamil society, despite all its eagerness to westernize itself through colonial forms of education, never ceased to be traditional in its awareness of and response to the sacred. And this is not to say that Tamil society was particularly religious, although religion does play a major part in the lives of the people. What is more important is that relationships, rituals, conventions, and even the landscape are framed by meanings that go beyond the rational and the pragmatic. That dimension is always captured or implied in the diction. In translation this subtext disappears, partly because the English language is not "native" to the land and partly because the readership often has limited access to the culture. In any translation, these constitute impediments and the present anthology is no exception. And yet the poems and the short stories do work, for they capture something of the depth of experience that makes this literature meaningful.

The collection here is clearly eclectic. The writers included here are important figures, often well known to the Tamil reading public. Several others, equally significant, would have found representation, but for the constraints of space. Some major authors who have written consistently for several decades, and whose works have inspired younger writers, have not found inclusion in this collection. Even the number of poems by individual poets tends to vary, again not because one is better than the other, but because translators tend to go with poems they are familiar with. The objective of the collection is, however, to make available in translation a substantial body of contemporary Tamil writing from Sri Lanka that reflects something of the literature's richness, its imaginative reach, and its depth of experience.

I would like to thank Pathmanaba Iyer, Nithianandan and Cheran for reading the introduction, and for their valuable suggestions.

WORKS CITED

Cheran, R. et al. ed. *Maranathul Vaalvom*. Coimbatore, India: Vidiyal, 1985.
Nuhman, M A and A Jesurajah ed. *Pathinoru Eelathuk Kavignarkal*. Madras: Cre-A, 1984.
Sivathamby, K. "50 Years of Sri Lankan Tamil Literature." *Frontline* 7 May 99: 97-99.

Ahalikai

MAHAKAVI

Indran descends*
from the celestial mount.
The embroidered shawl
that hides his fragrant chest
reflects the rays of the waning moon
and chirping insects abruptly cease.

The anklets silent on his floating feet
no pause in his majestic stride,
on grassy plains he touches the earth
and moves towards a warbling stream.

A bud that awaits the sun
he plucks;
then cups his hand and inhales deep.
This earthly joy
that blooms at morn and fades at dusk
he spurns but loves it too.

He reaches the stream and quenches his thirst.
Did this tasteless drink
defy the taste of celestial food?
A fleeting smile escapes his lips,
he flicks the flower and approaches the hut.

His shawl that seems to shine
like all the stars in the serene sky,
his sword, sandals, and bracelets too

1

he hides with care
and treads once more the declining path.

His piercing eyes gaze and search
the maze of trees,
the line of shrubs
he squints his eyes and sees the hut.

He steps across the thornless stile,
the fowls from branches
disturbed stare.
He moves with steadfast eyes
blind to all but a tiny
crack through which he peers.

Ahalikai moves her stalk-soft arms
across the hoary chest of sage Gothama;
he wakes, thinks it dawn
and leaves the hut—all these are watched.

The arm that slides to seek its joy
now comes back to rest
on half-seen breasts.
The lips curl with wistful smile
She sighs and turns.

Gothama leaves for his well-worn seat
his eyes close in meditative pose.
Indran stands at the foot of the bed
eyes aflame with burning passion;
he sees her squirm with love unfed.

No beast of prey would dare approach
this hut the sage had made his own.
Now he stands with boundless lust
his body aches, he takes a step!

Ahalikai

She gasps with pain, yet loves
the hands that hold with love;
he buries in her the passion he brought
she sees him not but feels the joy.

Like one possessed his lips seek
the eyelids and the sensual frame
his body hot he makes her his
as she gently opens her eyes.

She sees, shudders, breaks out in sweat
and seems to freeze and breathing stops.
And as she stares
becomes a stone.

The lord of all celestial beings
watches in horror the woman he craved.
The sage returns and glances around
strokes his beard and turns away.

Indran flees
damned for dateless time.
His body erupts in a thousand sores.
Deserted by all, a senseless stone
she waits for the touch of a godly foot.

Translated by Chelva Kanaganayakam

*This poem is based on a popular legend that Indran, the monarch of the angels, was once enamoured of a young and beautiful woman called Ahalikai, the wife of a sage called Gothama. One day, in order to seduce her, Indran descended to the earth in the early hours of the morning and crowed like a rooster outside Gothama's hut. The sage left, thinking it was dawn, and Indran entered the hut and seduced the unsuspecting Ahalikai. Gothama soon realized that he had been tricked, and returned in time to see Indran. He cursed them both, and Indran's body was studded with a thousand sores while Ahalikai was transformed into a stone. Long years later, she regained human form when the foot of Rama touched the stone.

Faster, Faster

NILAAVANAN

Faster, my dear carter, faster,
let's head for the new town
Before night falls.
    Faster, my dear, faster.

Love-drenched songs
resound in grove, field and flower.
Let's be done with journeying.
    Faster, my dear, faster.

Before the dew-tears' mournful curtain
glooms the path
before the sick moon's shadow dogs us,
    Faster, my dear, faster.

Translated by A J Canagaratna

Gently Flows the River

V I S JAYAPALAN

Scattered among the plains
here and there
fields are ploughed.
The din of machines
hardly dispels
the silence.

With hardly a ripple
the Pali river
flows gently.
The tall weeds
whisper to the winds
talk incessantly.
The birds
sing their music
and the fish
plop as they splash.

Still something sustains
the silence.
Beyond the bend
hidden by a rock
amidst the weeds
in the sand
where the marutha tree
shapes a fence,
filtering the light.
The winsome girls

from our village
gossip with relish
the village news
they laugh and giggle
tease and scold
wash and bathe.

Yet, silently
the river moves;
the footprints of
Panadara Vanniyan
are still visible.
Here he rested
conferred with his troops
planned his attack,
then washed his dusty feet
drank from the river,
content in the thought
of the retreating British
he rested awhile
shaded by the same
tree.

Beyond the bend
in the same enclave
the women
still bathe,
and with hardly a ripple
the river moves on.

Translated by Chelva Kanaganayakam

A Silver Anklet

ILANGAYARKONE

For one who desired nothing more than a sewing box and a container for the kitchen, the sheer quantity of fares displayed along the temple street was overwhelming. Small and large baskets with lids, woven baskets . . . unbelievable! She gently pinched her husband, who had untied the bull and was intently wiping the white foam from its mouth, rubbing it on its shiny black skin, and said, "Come on, let the bull be."

The last rays of the setting sun lit the top of palmyrah trees. Gradually the moon was rising in the east. This was the final day of the Vallipura temple's festival.

"Look at the crowd, how are we supposed to go through?" asked Nallamma as she edged closer to her husband.

Chelliah pulled off the cloth from his shoulder, tied it around his waist, and grabbed his wife's hand, saying, "Don't be scared, come with me."

Everything on the street and in the shops was a source of joy for Nallamma. She went on chattering endlessly. She felt that she should skip like a five-year-old, her skirt held high, showing her knees. Completely absorbed in his wife's elation, Chelliah let her drag him around.

He too was one of the men who toiled ceaselessly against the barren soil of Jaffna to make it yield a livelihood. The daily battle against the merciless land had made his body taut and sinewy. His sense of purpose made him silent.

It was three months ago that he had found a wife. Her chatter, her eyes that looked at him with so many unanswerable questions and her waist that seemed to break under the weight of her breasts seemed to infuse fresh life in his otherwise drab life. For one who tills the land

7

every day, the earth is full of secrets, fragrances and marvels. How many more secrets and surprises are hidden in life? How wonderful life is! What other evidence was needed than the forty-rupee reversible vetti that Chelliah was wearing today?

The crowds in the temple were yelling as they pleased. The babies cried. The priests kept hurrying back and forth. In the midst of all this activity the sound of the bell in the inner sanctum was heard. Palms placed together were lifted above the heads of people. Standing next to a pillar, Chelliah watched all this, his hands folded. Beside him, Nallamma, her hands raised above her head, struggled to get a glimpse of the deity. In the distance she saw the glitter of lamps. Beside them a dark priest with a huge belly was moving his hands. Beyond that—was that the God of Vallipuram?

The crowds, eager to receive the offering after the wedding of the God, now heard the drums starting up and shifted towards the musicians.

The drummer was completely absorbed in the myriad notes that issued from him. In rhythm with his disheveled kudumi-knot, a thousand heads began to shake. Nallamma found it amusing. Rubbing her body against her husband, she said, "They are all mad." His absorption broken, Chelliah replied, "Enough, let's go out."

On the streets outside, waves of people were moving around. On the white sand that looked like scattered pearls and diamonds, there was the glow of the moon as it embraced the night like the love of a newly pregnant woman, and the people from all parts of Jaffna were here, eager to shed the stress of the perpetual battle of life.

The owner of the sherbet shop ran a stick over his bottles, creating a music of his own. Seated beside a flickering lamp, his eyes peeled for the khaki uniform of policemen, the four-for-one man kept yelling, "Come on, come on, lose and it is money for peanuts, win and it is money for tea."

Without quite realizing it, Chelliah and Nallamma found themselves in front of a stall that displayed bangles. Nallamma loved the glitter of glass bangles in the light. Chelliah bought her five bangles. His eyes were then drawn to an unusual anklet in a glass case. From a tightly knit circle of silver hung ornamental spheres and a single piece shaped like a spear. A lion's face adorned the front. He had never seen one quite like this. He looked at his wife's face.

In the gas light her eyes seemed to widen and sparkle.

She didn't own even an ordinary anklet. Chelliah felt the urge to see this one on her smooth and rounded ankle. Several other images overcame him. He must buy the anklet for her. He asked the shop-keeper for the price.

"It's thirty-five rupees, and that's final."

Chelliah had all of thirty-one rupees tucked in his waist.

"I will give you twenty-five. Let me have that."

"Thamby! This is not worn by common people. This anklet is fit for a queen. It was imported from India. Look, this is not going to work. My final price is thirty rupees. Do you want it?"

"Alright, here . . ."

The anklet changed hands and found its way on to Nallamma's ankle.

Their feet sinking in the sand, the two of them went around the shops once more. With the remaining one rupee they bought a sewing box and a glass of sherbet each. They didn't buy the container for the kitchen.

Nallamma's legs ached. "Let's go and sit for sometime in the cart, finish the festival and leave at dawn," they decided. Chelliah guided her through throngs of people. Once the crowd cleared, Nallama suddenly lifted her foot and felt her ankle.

"God, the anklet is missing—"

"What? Look again carefully."

"It must have dropped off somewhere in the sand."

"Why can't you be a little more careful? You are far too flighty. Careless bitch!"

In the next instant Chelliah bit his tongue.

Nallamma's enthusiasm burst like a balloon. This was the first time in three months that she had been scolded, and that too in public! She was angry, ashamed and sad, tears filled her eyes.

"Enough of this temple visit with you. Let's go home."

Chelliah came down a notch. "Nallamma, I was angry when I said that. Listen . . ."

"No, we need to go now, get the cart. If you don't come I will walk by myself. On the way let me be run over by a car or bus."

Without a word, Chelliah grabbed the cart and brought the bull over. He was a man.

The bells on the necks of the bull tinkled as they stepped on the uneven road. Along the road that stretched out like a carpet spread out to receive a groom, the palmyrah trees on either side seemed to pay obeisance.

Having slackened the reins which went through the bull's nose, Chelliah placed his foot between its legs. The bull, intoxicated with pride, flew on the road. Should she be so angry because of a thoughtless word. He knows the value of money, having toiled and sweated in the tobacco farm. He was a man. He had a right to say a few things. Why shouldn't a woman bear that? After all, he spent all his money on her. He didn't buy even a cigar for himself.

Her legs swung over the back of the cart, Nallamma was deep in thought, her eyes fixed on the road beneath her. What pettiness!

It was all her fault. Without any difficulty they could have watched the rest of the festival and returned home happy. What if the husband said a few harsh words?

The bull panted with the effort. At the Nelliaddy intersection, Chelliah stopped the cart under a tree. Even at midnight, the shops were open for the benefit of those going to the temple. Two women were cooking appam. Apart from the clatter of tea being made in the shops, there was silence everywhere.

After stroking the bull to ease its fatigue, Chelliah walked towards the tea shop. Nallamma knew that he had only five cents. Following lunch he had had nothing to eat. He must be so hungry and yet hasn't said a word. She was anxious. Her heart melted. She recognized his nobility and the depth of his love for her. He remembered what he told her one day soon after their marriage: "Girl, I will give my life for you. You don't have to fear a thing."

Chelliah came back with a cigar, and placing a roll of betel by her side, looked into her eyes. Her face, streaked with tears, moved him. He wanted to wipe off her tears with his forty-rupee vetti.

"What is it, Nallam."

A shy smile now filled the tearful face. "Nothing. Aren't you hungry? Let's go home soon."

Chelliah understood what she meant. Once more the bells of the bull echoed on the street.

The Vallai plains!

As if the bull recognized the strength of this area, it slowed down to a steady walk.

A gust of wind whipped across the road.

The overcast sky seemed to hug the land. A stagnant pool in the middle of the plains shone like a jade on the chest of a giant. The moon on the horizon glowed weakly, eager to disappear.

On this plain that inspired grand thoughts even in the basest of people, the pulse of mankind continued to beat, untrammeled by the trappings of modernity.

Somewhere in the distance, a glow of light, two feet above the ground, moved steadily towards the road. As soon as he spotted it, Chelliah hawked and spat. "What's that?" Nallamma asked.

"Those are fishermen with their catch," lied Chelliah as he twisted the tail of the bull.

The light crossed the road, sped quickly and died.

Chelliah's left hand went towards his wife's waist.

His heart spread out like the plains of Vallai. He was overcome by a sense of joy. Raising his voice, he began to sing. He was not hungry, thirsty or sleepy. Nothing could harm him now, not even legions of Kollivai devils.

Translated by Chelva Kanaganayakam

Let's Chat in the Moonlight

N K RAGUNATHAN

The Right Honorable Sivapragasam had just returned home after addressing a temperance movement meeting that evening. He had appeared before the thousands gathered there and eloquently held forth in chaste Tamil about the evils of liquor, called for its total prohibition, and explained the ways of achieving this objective. He did not fail to weave in references to Gandhism in his oration

It was about eight pm. Not only was he hungry, he also felt tired. The flavours of his dinner still tickling his taste buds, he picked up the paper *One People* and came out to the verandah. Relaxing in the armchair in the corner, he began to read the paper under a dazzlingly bright light overhead.

Hardly had he finished a paragraph than he heard people conversing outside the gate. He turned towards them.

There were ten or twelve of them, poor workers by their looks. One of them hesitantly approached him. The others stayed where they were. Sivapragasam rose, took two steps forward and looked intently at the approaching man.

"Oh, is it you Kantha, what's the news?" he asked.

"We came to see you . . . it's the ban on liquor," was the diffident reply.

"Oh, is that so? Yes, let's talk about it," said Sivapragasam.

"Some others have come too. Let me call them," said Kantha turning towards the gate to beckon to the others to come in.

Sivapragasam was flustered, but only for a moment. Raising his eyebrows, scratching his head, he came to a snap decision.

"Kantha, don't call them. These are things that no outsider, not even the wife or children should know. These are dangerous times. Who knows what snake is lurking in which anthill? Look. It's a fine moonlit night. That heap of sand too is as white as milk. Come, let's go there and chat," he said.

Without waiting for a reply, he stepped down from the verandah and began to walk. Kantha followed.

Then, summoning those who stood at the entrance, they moved a short distance away, sat down in a convenient spot and began talking. The visitors were all from depressed castes. Toddy tapping was their livelihood. "Ban liquor" was the slogan resounding throughout the village. What was to be their fate then?

They too had listened to Sivapragasam's eloquence at the meeting. That was why they had come to discuss with him this subject that hit them in their very bellies.

"We, too, support prohibition. We know that liquor is a great menace. This livelihood doesn't give us much pleasure. The villagers curse us. Even after bribing the excise men we have to hide ourselves whenever they are sighted. Is that all? Every second we risk our lives, when we are aloft the trees that touch the sky . . . think of our state. A very precarious livelihood indeed. However . . .," said one of the young men present.

"Why do you hesitate? Tell us, Thamby," urged Sivapragasam.

"We need another livelihood."

Sivapragasam smiled. "What's so difficult about that? Surely in this wide world, there is no dearth of jobs."

"Yes, there are many. But are they for us?"

"Why?"

"If we open a tea shop, who will come to drink tea? If we open a grocery store, what's the guarantee they'll come to buy provisions from us? They are not prepared to give us a job even in a hardware store. They think our touch will pollute the hardware items. Let's not go any further. Are you prepared to employ me as a servant in your house? In such a situation . . . ," said the young man and looked at Sivapragasam's face. Sivaapragasam smiled and said, "Don't say that, Thamby. That's entirely different. Are these the only openings? You can take to some industry or other."

The youth was about to retort when a middle-aged man who had kept silent upto now stopped him and said angrily, "Yes, all these are entirely different matters to you. What do you care? You will say so many things; look at me. I am getting to be fifty years old now, by the time I become skilled in a job, it'll be time enough for Yama to throw his noose round my neck. When I'm learning the new job, will I be paid at all?. Till then my wife and children will have to starve. Isn't that your scheme?"

Sivapragasam sensed he was in a tight corner, but trying to brazen it out, he lamely said. "Don't get angry. Write and put forward your demands to the government, Instead of tapping toddy, tap sweet toddy. Ask the Minister of Industries to put up a sugar factory for you. I'm sure he'll pay heed."

A new insurgent voice made itself heard now.

"We don't want any of these. Whether alcohol is beneficial or harmful, our caste has begun to make some progress. That doesn't please you at all. That's why you want prohibition. Abolish liquor, snatch our livelihood in the name of Mahatma Gandhi. We will starve to death. Mahatma Gandhi said Untouchability should be abolished, didn't he? If we perish, then Untouchability will end, won't it? You hit two mangoes with one stone. At the same time, let gin and brandy be sold in pharmacies as medicine."

"No, no, this is a wrong-headed argument. You shouldn't think like that at all."

"What else are we to think? Using Gandhi's name, you have set out to abolish liquor. Shouldn't you abolish Untouchability first?" the voice retorted.

Sivaprgasam was petrified. He hadn't foreseen this outburst. Those who had come got up to leave.

"We'll get going. Ponder well and do the right thing. Liquor should be banned, no doubt. At the same time we should be able to lead a happy life. Act on this basis, and we too will join you in your campaign," they said as they left.

It didn't take them long to fathom why Sivapragasam had said, when they arrived, "It's a fine moonlit night outside. Let's chat in the moonlight."

Translated by A J Canagaratna

Passion

M A NUHMAN

Within my heart
and every pore,
lie unplucked
in a splendid heap
a thousand buds
in the tree of youth.

The flower of passion
as is its wont
blooms in plenty
and fades away.

The fallen leaves fade
new flowers bloom
to take their place.
The blown petals fall
and fade once more.

The flower still fresh
I yearn to give;
no soft hand
to touch to take,
as my days
drew heavily on.

You came to dispel
you stood waiting
all alone;

the fragrance of a flower
newly bloomed
those eyes expressed.

To meet is nothing
but was this long
awaited meeting
just one more?

Within your heart
in every pore
lie unplucked
a thousand buds.

The flower of passion
as is its wont
blooms in plenty
and fades away.

All these within
you wanted to give.
just like me
you too waited
interminable days
for someone to come.

The rightness of mingling
two hearts
locked and yearning
you revealed to me.
The joy of mingling
two hearts
locked and yearning
you revealed to me.

Your flower

your fragrant thought
you granted to me
your full red lips.
Your mellow lips
plucked
the passion within.
As each moment
grew and blossomed,
the fruits of your breast
pressed on my chest,
those fleeting moments
are fresh in my mind.

I stepped across
the open door,
into your house.
My lips grew wet,
they still are moist;
your lips so soft
lie impressed
upon my lips.

To meet is nothing
to meet and part
that too is nothing.

In my dreams
in my thoughts
you come and depart.
In your dreams
in your thoughts
sometimes I too
might come and depart.

You and your thoughts
the load of your thoughts

like lengthening shadows
in fading dusk,
grow in my mind
and burden my heart.

Translated by Chelva Kanaganayakam

The Chariot

S PONNUTHURAI

The ritual of Arumugam (also known as Mukathar) waking up is a spectacle in itself. The way he rolls up his mat, having placed his pillow and sheet in it, is an art. A yawn like the howl of a fox, hands stretched out above the head and then folded back down, an elaborate body stretch, and the ritual comes to an end. By his pillow there is always a box of matches and a roll of tobacco. Once the cigar is lit, his feet automatically start moving in the direction of the back yard. He himself hardly remembers when this practice began.

He has lived for over sixty years. Without the benefit of a watch, he functions with more precision than the hands of a clock. His morning ablutions completed in the backyard, having washed himself, he then cleans his teeth with the burnt chaff kept in a coconut shell that hangs from the kamuku tree, before returning to the verandah. From the white shell he pinches out a little holy ash with the fingers of his right hand, and as he mutters "Siva Siva" the sound of the Nallur temple announcing the morning pooja is inevitably heard.

Now, as he hears the temple bells sounding the pooja, Mukathar says to himself, "Today is New Year."

So many New Years have come and gone, and with them so many years have vanished. The New Year in the first year that Parvathipillai got married; after the vow in Rameswaram, the birth of Murugan, the shaving of his head in Murugandy, and the New Year the following day; Sountharam's marriage and the first New Year with her husband; having lit the funeral pyre for his father, the New Year of abstinence; the death of Parvathipillai and the New Year during a time of deep despair; so many of these—the years that consumed his life and caused his body to shrink. He no longer possesses the energy of the past. Three servings of Pittu with brinjals fried in sesame seed oil and four baked manioc pieces with green chillies to feed his hunger—these are memories of his youth. Restricting himself to only two slices of bread because the children had to be educated is a habit that is now practiced in his house as well. There is really nothing wrong with him, he is not sickly. Just the onset of old age. He feels the pain of mild arthritis. Standing up quickly is now a strain. And yet he tries to avoid letting his children notice the changes. His only worry now is his youngest daughter.

He sits in the verandah and leans against the post.

"A pity about this child. She destroyed the mother. Now that she has finished her studies, she sits in a corner and sighs all day. It is true that the older siblings want her to study further. If they want to, let them get their daughters to study. The younger son is alright. Somehow he has managed to find a job. They say he works in a company. Apparently the salary is good. There is the possibility of moving up, according to the older son and his cousins. As the youngest, he is used to eating at home. For three or four months he had to manage without that. A little struggle now will teach them how to live their lives later. Thanks to the Nallur Murugan, all the children seem capable of looking after themselves. It has nothing to do with me – it is all up to God. The older son will arrive by the morning train. Even if he forgets or can't be bothered, his wife Kamala will want to come. She believes in the Kaiviyalam from me. Their oldest child—these fashionable names are difficult to remember—she must be over ten years old. She might even be eleven. Almost the age of puberty—ever her mother's death feels like yesterday. Almost five years have passed. She is a lucky woman—she has gone, leaving all the burden on my shoulders."

Suddenly he remembers the letter from Manoharan. He says he needs to return to Colombo on New Year's day itself.

"That too is right. Our ways are not good forever. He has just joined this new place of work and shouldn't be spoiling his good name by asking for leave.

"Oh Muruga."

The door of the small room opens and the youngest, Padma, comes out.

"Sure, she has grown up, but at home she is still a small girl. She looks so much like Parvathipillai. If I can get her settled, that is all I need. I can then close my eyes. For Manoharan, maybe my brother-in-law's daughter would be a possibility. With boys it is difficult to be sure."

Padma first sweeps the yard and sprinkles water mixed with cow dung over it. Even before the dawn of New Year, the desire to finish her daily rituals is evident, the belief that if everything gets done without a fault on New Year's day, the whole year will be as faultless. Old curries are not in demand on this day. Having taken all the pots to the shade of the king coconut tree, she scrubs them with a coir brush and then washes them. She notices her father seated on the verandah, immersed in thought. As she tries to scrape off the burnt food from the bottom of a pot, she begins,

" Appu . . . will anna be coming by the morning train?"

"Yes daughter . . . it won't be New Year without Subramaniam. Whatever happens, surely he won't fail to come today."

"He will come for sure. Kamala will drag him by his ear if necessary. The train won't have reached Navatkuli by now. If I start walking now, I can reach the station. But then he doesn't like that. 'No one needs to show me the way to our house'—that is always his angry response."

"Daugher, have you lit the fire to make tea?"

"Yes."

"Has your sister Parimalam got up yet? Your brother-in-law too came in late. He wouldn't have eaten properly."

His daughter Parimalam's husband also works in Colombo. Parimalam came to the father's house for Thai Pongal and did not return to Colombo. Her husband Sathasivam arrived by Yal Devi last night.

"God has given them everything. They have even spent thirty thousand on building a new house. They will probably move to the new house in June. For sure, they are not going to live there forever. They will rent it out. They seem to have bought a car as well, although they have never brought it to Jaffna. Despite all their kindness and generosity God has not given them a child. According to the

21

horoscope childbearing will happen somewhat late. Even Sathasivam was born after seven years. All the specialists in Colombo have been consulted. They have not found a problem."

"Drink the coffee before it gets cold," Padma hands him the glass.

"You have made egg coffee. Your brother-in-law is here. Subramaniam will be here soon. His Asokan loves eggs."

"We have plenty of eggs. We can even fry them for Pittu."

Mukathar drinks his coffee.

"Daughter, Sountharam was here yesterday. What did she tell you? Will she be here for lunch?"

"Athan came home yesterday. His sister and family—from Parangi Street—are going to be with them for lunch. Evening is likely to be convenient for them. But she will send Mukunthan for the Kaiviyalam.

"Sountharam has a large family. But she is something else. She is educating all her six children. I didn't give her much by way of dowry. Her husband Thangaraja is really a generous man. For the sake of their education he has left the family behind and gone to Colombo by himself. There he lives a frugal life, eating food in restaurants. To afford the cost of running two homes, he works in another place after office hours. At that age one needs to run around and work. But you need the right food as well. Fortunately, the daughters are young. That's a relief. After all, instead of cooking for her husband, she is not going to rush over here. Daughters belong to us only until they are married.

"Daughter, give me my purse and my Salvai."

"Are you going to the store this early?"

"No just up to the intersection. Maybe I will get something."

Having tied his sarong firmly around himself, his purse tucked in and his Salvai wrapped around his shoulder, he crosses the gate.

In the midst of all of his tender thoughts, there is a little thorn of discomfort, evident in the mechanical movement of his feet. Pasupathy from the shop at the intersection calls him.

"Annai, how are you? At what time does the New Year begin? At what time does one get Kaiviyalam, and what is the auspicious time to begin work?" Having asked at least ten people, he is still not sure.

"Ten twenty-eight is when New Year begins. For Kaiviyalam no specific time has been mentioned. But the day is alright, so there is no harm in giving it at the same time."

Mukathar is meticulous about reading the almanac. For a man who does not own a watch, he has the knack of telling you accurately all the auspicious times.

"I never really bother about these days and times. Starting on New Year is fine, isn't it? Otherwise it drags on. There is no auspicious time for two or three days, and am I supposed to keep my shop closed?"

"Oh yes, it is all a matter of belief Pasupathy," says Mukathar. "Looks as if the train hasn't arrived," he changes the topic.

"It is late . . . With the number of people traveling at New Year, the train tends to be late. From what I hear, your other son Kumaraswamy is also coming today. I haven't seen him in a while."

The thorn in his heart nestles gently in the bed of petals.

Mukathar doesn't know of Kumaraswamy's visit. No one expects him on any formal occasion. It is just his nature. Even so, Mukathar does not betray his surprise at Kumaraswamy's intended visit.

"Here, did you see this flier? The Tamil society is having its annual function. They say it includes plays as well. Apparently Kumaraswamy is going to be their chief guest."

Pasupathy hands over the flier.

Mukathar has some difficulty reading nowadays. Still he identifies his son's name, mentioned in bold letters. His heart warms. And yet without a change of expression he returns the flier.

"My eyes are blurry"

"Shall I read it to you?"

"No, Pasupathy. I have to go. It looks as if my older son has just passed by in his car."

Although the older son serves as an excuse to leave, Mukathar continues to think of Kumaraswamy. He is Mukathar's second son. He studied hard and advanced quickly.

With all his brains, should he be like this? He should have studied in England and should be owning two or three cars and four or five houses. They would say that the evil eye fell on him. Sountharam got a husband on the strength of Subramanian. A husband for Parimalam was achieved by mentioning the name of Kumaraswamy.

When those same tongues turned against him and branded him . . .

"Ripe before his time. With two older brothers and two young girls still unmarried, his craving for marriage. And that too to a Christian of no standing. His education is fit to clean one's tongue with. Let him throw his education away and carry a bucket of night soil!"

When such words burnt the hairs on his chest and seared his heart, so many stoked the fire. All those who brought sweets and tea and betel for the mildest of headaches and fevers, now, after Kumara-swamy's hasty marriage, shunned his gate. Subramaniam was of course a source of comfort, but even so Mukathar felt that in this big world he had been abandoned and left alone.

"What can we do, either of us? It all happens as it was meant to be. He did it out of some foolishness. Now do we cut off a finger of our own? Swallowing my pride, I visited them once. She is not bad. That she had integrity was clear from her face. For his personality, he would love someone like her. So what if she is a Christian? How many have fallen into the pit, having looked at caste and creed? After all, does he go to the temple regularly? Or use holy ash? He seems to have prevented her from going to the temple as well. He looks skinny, but is really stubborn. Just because she is Parvathy, is she any less stubborn? He is different, and no one really understands him. 'Those who hide behind fences and live against their conscience will not understand me. I know what I am doing!' he once shouted. I can't blame them either. Why associate with one who doesn't go with the flow? Why do I need to be friends with those who avoid me, was his argument. His three children are supposed to be very bright. I would really like to see them. When he came for the anniversary of my wife's death he brought his son with him. The son refused to get off my lap, holding a banana and calling me 'appappa.' Three functions alto-gether—Pongal, New Year and Deepavali—and he does not show up for any one of these. Sometimes on a rare day he comes by himself and talks about his children. He goes to the kitchen to get himself something to eat. Saying he has meetings here and there, he leaves.When I inquire later I find that he left by the next train. It's true, no one here understands his ways. They don't care for his ways either. There is a measure of anger in their hearts. The ash of the sibling love they felt for him now covers that anger. Everyone at home speaks ill of him except me. After all, he too is my son. These people go their way, and he goes his. Do all five fingers look the same? These people are foolish, despite all their education. I bore them for the sake of having a family. A family moves like a chariot. I bore him for the village. Let's assume he does nothing useful. And these ones do not like my praising him. They think my loyalty is with him. 'Whatever you say, he too is my child,' I tell them. They are no saints. They behave as if I've said that only he was my child. Mothers are always partial. She is no longer alive and I am partial. There is one thing about Kumaraswamy that I will never forget. Let them say a thousand things. Let it be Subramaniam, Soundaram, Parimalam, Manoharan or Padma; all of them are known as Mukathar Arumugam's children. Why even with Sathasivam and Thangarajah—they too are best known as my sons-in-law. Do they know how many on the street know me as Kumaraswamy's father? The other day when I was in a bus on my way to Tellipallai, a young boy asked me 'Aren't you Kumaraswamy's father?' and gave me his seat. That boy too must be an educated one."

"Mukathar, have all your sons arrived?" Aiyambadi inquires from his gate.

"The train must have arrived some time ago."

"Subramaniam won't stay away; is Manoharan coming too?"

"Yes, so he wrote."

"Why are you talking from the entrance? I just wanted to have a drop of something before going to the store—but don't you know my wife? It has to be for someone else's sake. Why don't you come in?"

"I have arthritic pains . . . it doesn't agree with me anymore."

"This is not everyday, Mukathar. It's only for New Year. Even when I saw you in the distance, I felt I had to begin the New Year with you."

"Well, why ruin your wish?"

Having joked around with Aiyampillai, he then went to the store with him and bought vegetables and fruits for his children and grandchildren and when he returned it was almost ten o'clock.

25

The house was in a festive mood. With Subramaniam's family around, noise was never in short supply. The children were dressed in new clothes.

"I got held up spending time with Aiyampillai. Subramaniam appears to have chosen the same colour for all the children's clothes. Look, this tiny tot claims his clothes are the best. . . . Parimalam and Sathasivam have had their bath. These clothes are expensive. They always buy such clothes for New Year. Now they are ready to go to the temple. Muruga, give this family a child! Really, touch wood, this sari is pretty on Padma. Having worn a sari first when she attained puberty, it is only now that she has written to Manoharan asking for a beige sari. He must have bought it. Subramaniam and Kamala have not finished their bath—they are at the well."

"Padma, take these vegetables into the kitchen."

"Appu, you went to the store before having breakfast. I fried an egg and waited for you."

"Aiyampillai would't let me leave. It was just as well that I went to the store with him. The meat I got was excellent. The little ones won't eat if the food is hot. I bought liver for a mild curry. The son-in-law doesn't eat meat. I bought very good Para fish for him. The rest should be good for a fried curry. If I had waited to finish the Kaiviyalam, I wouldn't have got a thing at the store."

Padma carries the bag with some difficulty to the kitchen, saying, "Appu's New Year has begun on an auspicious note."

"This vetti is for Pethappa," announces Asokan as he puts a vetti on the table. "Chittappa also bought a vetti with a border for appa," he adds. "I tried but Parimalam wouldn't listen. Yesterday she got a paramas pair." Asokan piled all the clothes together and said, "Four vettis for Pethappa this year."

"It is actually three vettis and one Salvai," corrects Hamsathoni from a corner.

"Unnecessary expense. They never listen. They like to do things for me. When Manoharan was living at home, he would wear all these clothes. Now he too has started buying for me. It is only Soundaram's son Mukunthan who might wear them. He too will take the GCE exam this year."

Kamala runs into her room in her wet sari. Subramaniam, standing beside the clothes line in the front yard, drying his hair says, "Appu, the Maruthu water is by the well. Finish your bath."

"What's the hurry? Let Manoharan bathe first. Where is he?"

"These kids wanted ice cream from sugar, Chithappa, and he has gone to get it for them. Let him bathe later. You go first. It is almost time for New Year and we need to place the Kumbam."

"Alright," Mukathar goes to the well. He usually bathes in the sarong he has on. Once a week is the special Saturday bath. He sprinkles marutha water liberally on his head.

"Chithappa! Chithappa!" Asokan is jubilant.

"Has Kumaraswamy arrived?"

He looks out eagerly. The leaves of the touch-me-not droop.

"No, it's Manoharan. In three or four months, how he has grown. Earning your own money makes a difference. He spends freely. It's only a few months since he left. The habits of Colombo have not rubbed off on him. Kumaraswamy is not to be seen. Would he have stayed back, thinking he should not make things awkward on an auspicious day?"

As this thought settles in, the thorn that gently pricked in the morning pierces further. He struggles with the pain. A sigh escapes him. Rapidly he draws water from the well and pours it over his head.

"I have come at the right time. Everyone appears to have finished their Marutha water bath. Padma, give this to the children."

"That is definitely Kumaraswamy's voice. This voice, distinctive as a bull's, is definitely his."

The water getting into his ears, gives shape to the thoughts in the recesses of his heart. Still he is drawn by desire.

"Where is Appu?"

"He is bathing . . . Appu, Sinnanna is here."

As his hope kindles, he looks over the enclosure of the bathing space.

Kumarswamy, smiling, is in the yard. By his side is Padma, giving the biscuits to the children. He notices Subramaniam's youngest child, scared by the presence of the stranger, hiding behind a chair. "I am a Chithappa too, has no one told you?" says Kumaraswamy, smiling.

The same laugh. His laugh won't change; nor will his curly hair that sticks up in a tuft at the front. Whatever resentment there is, no one has the heart to scold him when he laughs. It charms everyone.

"You couldn't send a postcard to let us know that you were coming?" Mukathar chides him.

"It's all a rush, Appu. Why do you need a postcard—here I am in person. Anyway, Padma is wearing a sari." He looks at her, seeing her in a sari for the first time.

"Yes, Manoharan bought it for her from his first month's salary," Mukathar says.

"Where is Athan Padma? Did he drive?"

"No, he took the Uttaradevi last night. He is at the temple with Acca," says Padma, going towards the kitchen.

"Heard he bought a new car. What make is it?"

"How would I know about these things?"

"Do you know how expensive cars are these days? That chap in the other house—Ratnagopal—sold his car and bought a scooter."

"From what I hear, he did not sell his car. He bought a scooter as well."

"It is not possible to buy anything these days. That is why he sold it. Rasathotta Sangarapillai bought his car. How are his marriage proposals?"

"That is all a mess."

"You are talking about the proposal from Manipay. This one is from Kopay."

"I didn't hear about that one."

He looks at Manoharan, who was leaning against a post: "Thambi, I am told that the government is going to take over your company. Then you will become a government servant."

"That won't happen."

"You wait and see, Thamby. Appu, Thangarajah Athan is going to get a promotion next month—did you hear?"

"How would I know these things?"

"Two days ago when I dropped him off at the station on my bike, that is when he told me," Manoharan adds.

"He comes very rarely to the village, and yet he knows just about everything that happens here."

Mukathar hurries through his bath and dries himself.

"Did you hear about the Anaikoddai doctor's daughter?" he asks, coming up.

"Yes I heard. They jumped up and down about the caste. He is a good boy—he teaches at Kelakathara."

"They said something like that."

As he dries his hair, he thinks about what to wear. Nothing trivial about the decision. He is concerned that none of his children feel slighted or hurt.

"Why are you with your wet clothes . . . here, wear this. It the kind of blue sarong that you like," he stretches out a package.

Not even the god Krishna, eating the food given by Kuselan, could be happier.

He spreads it out and puts it on.

Without the slightest anxiety, he looks at the others.

Silence.

"It looks good on Appu," Padma dispels the silence.

"Have you come from a place where you stand all the time? Sit down. I am going to place the Kumbam. Since it is a neutral day, I am going to give the Kaiviyalam."

"No, Appu. You know I don't believe in these things. Not only that, I got my Kaiviyalam from the cab driver this morning."

Mukathar's face clouds over.

"He belongs to a different mould," Subramaniam, who has been quiet all this while, interjects. "No belief in anything. You, your books, the stories and plays you write do not educate you. What you get from everywhere is not wisdom. What you learn at home is wisdom. To do as the people do is wisdom."

"It's not that, brother. I have come with five or six others. It's on other people's money that I have brought them here. They are new to the village. It doesn't look right for me to leave them in the hotel and stand around here. I'll get going." He turns away without waiting for a reply.

Whatever happens, he is respectful. Whoever speaks he listens with his head lowered. All that as a sign of respect, and yet he does what he wants.

"Chinanna, here is some coffee . . . drink it," Padma hands him a glass. Without a word he drinks the coffee and returns the glass.

As he plucks mango leaves for the Kumbam, Mukathar asks: "Will you be here for lunch?" There is hope in his tone.

"He has told us that he can't leave his friends."

Subramaniam doesn't always talk this way.

"Goodbye to all," says Kumaraswamy as he hurriedly opens the gate, and then pauses. "Appu, our play will be performed this evening in the open-air theatre . . . it should be good, come if you can."

Having set up the Kumbam, he gives out the Kaiviyalam. On the couch in the verandah, Subramaniam and Sathasivam are chatting. The conversation revolves around the car which Sathasivam has bought. A little further way there is Mukunthan, who has joined in on behalf of Soundaram.

"He is very respectful to his older uncle."

Kamala, Parimalam and Padma are busy in the kitchen. Hamsathoni runs around pretending to be older than she is. Seated on a plank, Manoharan is telling them about his experiences in Colombo.

The coconuts having been turned into 'por' coconuts, the game is in full swing in the yard. Asokan, by nature, will disrupt the game, claiming that his coconut broke because it hit a stone.

All the new clothes given to him by his children are on the table. Mukathar scans them.

"Padma."

She drops what she is doing and comes over.

"Put these clothes away, daughter. In the evening I have to go and see a play and I want to wear the vetti given by Muthanna and the salvai given by Athan."

"I feel sorry for Ilyannai."

"Yes, daughter. It is even better to be born in poverty than to be born the youngest," Manoharan says.

For some strange reason, Anna and Athan seem hugely amused. Manoharan picks up a piece of firewood and goes to a corner of the kitchen.

"Now thamby is also like the grownups," comments Parimalam.

"Parimalam, keep quiet. Just because he is the youngest doesn't mean that he should always be small. He too works and earns," says Kamala on behalf of her cousin.

"Manoharan has started to smoke. I can see the smoke. Well, once they are grown up, it's up to them."

"Nephew? It's science, isn't it? Don't neglect English."

"He is good in English. He should get a credit," Sathasivam assures him on behalf of his son.

"Are you holding up the post? Sit in that chair."

"Athan, if he stands there, I think he gets to see Hamsathoni working in the kitchen."

"Sathasivam . . . you were too late for Vanathi . . . you can try to succeed for Asokan."

Sathasivam looks in the direction of Parimalam and Kamala signals to Subramaniam to keep quiet.

Mukathar picks up a ginger biscuit from the verandah floor, and with childlike slyness crunches it between his old teeth.

Translated by Chelva Kanaganayakam

Shoes

DOMINIC JEEVA

When the burning sensation from his sole reached his head, Muthu
Mohamed lost his balance. He lifted his left foot and hopped like
someone performing the dance of Shiva.

With his thick lips and a stern face, he looked like a man afflicted
with epileptic fits.

Ah, if I could only get a pair of slippers.

Muthu turned and looked at the tarred road behind him. He saw a
wisp of smoke curling up from a cigarette butt. The moment he
looked at it, it was emitting its last puff of smoke. The pain from his
burning sole was not completely abated. His heart too felt the heat.

Semma Lane, whose name was mistakenly construed by the municipal
members as having a racial connotation, was later renamed Jumma
Mosque Lane because of a mosque which was built at one end of it. It
was only when Muthu Mohamed reached the top of this famous lane
and turned into Kasthuriar Road that he performed his divine dance.

Muthu held on to a telephone post, planted his right foot firmly on
the ground, raised his left leg up and gazed down at his singed sole.
Cigarette ash the size of a one-cent coin was stuck on to it. He took
some spit from his mouth and applied it there a few times. This first
aid was not very successful. The burn was still hurting. The stench
from the neighbouring drain made him feel nauseous too. He put his
left foot on the ground and, with a mixture of saliva and sand on the
burn, applied some pressure.

Muthu Mohamed was returning after the noon prayers at the
mosque. In his worried mind, the Ethul Alka festival of the following
day had turned into a frightful genie that increasingly bothered him.

His head, which should have had a cap, was covered and tied with a folded handkerchief. Two corners of the cloth flapped in the air.

His thoughts now changed direction. Today is Friday. The next morning will be the Haj Festival. Relieved from the pain on his sole, he directed his thoughts towards the next day's festival.

Muthu wanted to cross the road. He paused, wondering whether a car or another vehicle might suddenly come by. A blue car passed him and stopped just beyond the top of the road. Two young girls with very modern looks jumped off the car. Giggling, they mumbled something to each other. Between their parted lips, their teeth shone like artificial ones. One of the girls hurriedly entered a Shoe Palace nearby. The other, moving coolly, placed her foot on the first of the steps into the store when a pair of modern shoes in the showcase caught her eyes and held them. One leg on the first step and the other on the second, the young girl moved rhythmically, like a frog. Muthu Mohamed, appreciating the ultramodern dress and hairstyle of this girl, moved his eyes gradually down and stopped at her feet, the toes painted with cutex. The eyes stayed rooted on those flowery feet. All his thoughts were frozen on the brand new shoes she was wearing.

Muthu came to his senses. His mind went back to the ladies' shoes which had been exactly like these was looking at. His mind returned to the girl's feet before him. He closed his eyes a moment, when a state-owned bus rumbled along the street. The noise disturbed his thoughts and he moved to the edge of the road.

The little town was bustling with activity and Kasturiayar Road was like the main artery from the heart. This road was functioning actively as usual. The thought of the shoes came back to Muthu Mohamed. The girl, who had surrendered her mind to the shoes in the showcase, took another step up and entered the shop.

After all, this was just a pair of shoes for one's feet. It was a pair of ladies' shoes like this one that had been the cause of agony to Muthu's heart since that morning. He had never experienced or even known about such agony. He converted all this pain into a deep breath and heaved a sigh, perhaps expecting his torture to be relieved by such a sigh. But the tension in his heart was in no way reduced. He walked back to his shop with his heavy heart. Thirty steps southwards would take him to his shop. Calling it a shop would be an exaggeration. A pigeon nest would be a more appropriate term. While all other buildings were turning into multistoried ones with the coming of "civilization," his little shop still remained a third-rate workshop giving new life to torn and damaged shoes. The rent was only thirty rupees a month. Anyway, he was the proprietor, the great Muthu Mohamed. He was an expert worker and he was in great demand in the bazaar area. Although he was a young person, he knew the intricacies of his profession. He had a young boy as his assistant.

Muthu came in and took his seat in the workshop at eight in the morning and would get up at noon, for his meals and for his prayers. Seated with his back against the wall of his shop, he would watch the faces and feet of the people going along the road with frustration. This was his daily routine.

It was during one of these moments that a Malayan pensioner, a new customer, came to him. Muthu concluded that his new customer was a Malayan pensioner when he began with the words, "During my good old days in Singapore."

It was fifteen days ago that this customer brought a pair of English ladies shoes wrapped in a thick brown paper. He carefully opened the parcel and placed them on the workshop plank.

"Son, I got these in Singapore. Look here, a strap has given way. The other needs two nails; that's all. Can you mend these?"

Muthu examined them carefully, conducting his tests by pulling the straps and moving them in all directions.

"Yes, take a seat. I'll finish the job now itself. A piece of leather has to be sewed on one. The heel of the other has to be hammered in with a nail. This won't take long. Give me a rupee for the job."

"Make it reasonable. I'll give you seventy-five cents. But the work must be good. Do you understand?"

The bargaining was over. "Alright, just be seated here. I'll complete the job in a minute."

"Do I have the time to sit here? I'll walk around the town. You finish the job and keep the shoes."

"Alright, return soon. The shoes will be ready when you come."

The man went away and did not return that day. Nor did he return the following day, or the day after . . .

No, the customer did not come back at all.

The festival was nearing and a selfish desire brewed in Muthu's mind.

That useless fellow will not return. Who will benefit by keeping those shoes here? Such thoughts began to creep into Muthu's mind. He made a bold decision. Two days to go for the Haj festival . . . Many days have passed, what right does he have to ask for them? If I could only give them to Rageela as a gift, after giving them a few more final touches . . .

The mere thought of Rageela made his heart throb with delight.

Not even a year had passed since their marriage and now the Haj festival was around the corner.

Muthu had been wondering what gift he to give his Rageela, and while worrying about this the pensioner had come to his mind, and the shoes he had brought for repairs and forgotten to collect.

Rageela is not a greedy girl at all. But what about my status in the lane? If the women on this lane do not respect my Beebi, will she respect me? On the Haj festival day all the women of the area will meet for prayers in the big house at the corner of the lane. If on that day my Beebi does not look respectable, will these women respect us?

Muthu's desire turned into action. He kept up all night, used his deftness to make the Lady Ballerina shoes look like new. "Oh dear, look at the shape of these shoes now," he said to himself.

It was only yesterday that he had presented the shoes to Beebi and received great satisfaction. That thought itself gave him pleasure. His face reflected the sweet sensation that his mind had experienced. He laughed to himself like a madman. The image of the smiling face of Rageela brought him immense joy. All the sweet sensations of the world had been at his feet yesterday.

But today?

As if he had planned it, the pensioner had arrived at his shop this morning.

"Have you repaired the shoes I gave you?"

At that time only the boy was in the shop. Muthu Mohamed was not present. He was having a cup of tea in the tea boutique across the road and enjoying a beedi smoke. He let out the smoke through his mouth and nose. As he identified the pensioner in his shop, he hastily retreated through the rear of the tea shop and vanished.

But could he stay away from the shop the whole day?

Tomorrow is the Haj festival. There is a load of work at hand. Only if I make some money can I celebrate the festival. With these thoughts in mind Muthu Mohamed walked toward his shop.

If I could take those damn things and throw them at his face? But this was the first gift I gave her after the wedding. Tomorrow is the festival. Will it be nice for me if she does not wear those shoes and goes for prayers? . . . Alright, let today pass. Tomorrow the shop will be closed. The day after I could return the shoes.

Muthu argued with his conscience in this manner and the sad feelings faded away. But, like the spider which gets trapped in its own web, he too comforted himself in the web of his own thoughts.

Muthu Mohamed did not realize that he had already stepped into his workshop and taken his seat. The boy kept a pair of adult shoes and a pair of children's slippers before him and said, "A trousered gentleman gave these to be repaired. He wanted the heels to be attended to. He said he would return soon."

"Alright, you go home and return after lunch."

He began working like a machine in order to control his inner feelings. He had been accustomed to this work day in and day out. His mind was wondering like a stag roaming about in the jungle.

Muthu finished fixing the heel on one of the boots. He took the other one and removed the nails with a pair of pliers. The pliers slipped and with a jerk his elbow struck the wall. There was a slight pain. Beads of perspiration rose on his face. The hair on his head fell and covered his forehead. He pushed it back with his fingers, lifted the bottom of the cloth he was wearing and wiped his face.

His work continued.

The boots were polished and he had done a clean job. Next, he had to tackle the children's slippers.

"Look here, how many times have I to come in search of you?" It was a familiar voice.

Muthu raised his head and looked up. Oh, this good for nothing fellow. He sat home all these days and has come back to pester me, thought Muthu.

The Malayan pensioner began climbing the steps one by one. His figure was rising gradually. Muthu Mohamed had the feeling of having stepped on hot sand. A shock wave ran through his spine. There was silence for some time.

"Here, you, lift your head and look at me!"

Muthu looked up and then turned away his head. His heart trembled like the tail of a little lamb.

"Give me the pair of slippers I gave you that day."

"When was the due date?"

"I told you that I would return that day itself, but I couldn't. So I have come today. So get the slippers." The man took his purse and selected a twenty-five cent coin and a fifty-cent one.

Muthu Mohamed chose his words and gave a sharp reply. "When you don't come on the due date, the slippers are not here. They are in the trash." There was a tremble in his voice. A shade of fear was also there The customer did not expect this.

During the good old colonial days I hoodwinked even the powerful British. Now, this puny little fellow is trying to cheat me, thought the pensioner.

Nevertheless he did not express his anger in any manner. "What? Are you joking? That was a brand new pair of slippers. You say that you threw that pair of slippers I bought for eighteen rupees?"

"There is no point in your shouting. When I say that I have thrown them, I mean just that. Now what do you want me to do?" This time there was a tone of false anger in Muthu's voice.

Although the man had difficulty in controlling his anger, he said, "What, man, why are you telling me such a big lie? Can you swear that you threw away those slippers? Could you swear upon the very mother who delivered you that you threw away those slippers?"

"I swear upon my umma that I threw them."

"Would you swear upon your father that you threw them?"

"I swear upon my vappa that I put them in the trash."

"Oh!" The man was shocked beyond words. The situation was beyond reason.

This man is determined to cheat me. The man's feelings burned him as if he had swallowed solid fire.

"Oh, swear upon your God," he shouted. He actually screamed. Saying this, he climbed the steps further and stood on the plank that formed the narrow platform in the workshop.

"Yes, upon my God, I swear that I threw away those slippers."

What, this rascal swears upon his own God, the man thought to himself. He stood there like a soldier on a battlefield, having lost all his weapons. He felt that the whole world had let him down. He wondered if it would be wiser to save his self-respect than seek justice. With foolish stubbornness he looked here and there. Nothing came to mind.

Suddenly, like a streak of lightning a bright idea hit him. He removed the slippers he was wearing.

Let's see what this man is trying to do, thought the cobbler. But the words uttered by the pensioner fell clearly upon his ears.

"Now, this is the last chance, go ahead and touch these slippers, the very things that give you your daily bread, and swear upon them that you really threw those slippers in the trash."

Muthu lowered his eyes and looked at the orphaned pair of slippers. His conscience questioned him. Do I have to swear upon these, that give my daily bread?

There was silence.

The cobbler shook his head from side to side.

"No, I cannot swear upon these," said Muthu Mohamed.

Translated by S Thirunavukarasu

The Destitute Heart

A JESURASA

Half the day was spent sleeping off the weariness of travel by the night mail train. Even after lunch he snoozed, reclining in an easy chair.

Someone seemed to tap him on the shoulder and he came awake. His elder sister was standing there with a cup of tea. His younger brother too, it seemed, had come back from fishing: he was in the kitchen, eating.

My, it's past four o'clock. He was in a hurry.

"Where do you want to go?" elder sister asked.

To the *uppumal kanthor*. I can watch the boys play football."

The *uppumal kanthor*, football, and the boys. Oh, the evenings. My feet were itching to play but no, it's too tiring. It's nearly a year since I last played football . . . Damned Colombo . . . can't even play football."

He's cycling after a long time and the breeze makes it difficult for him to pedal. The monsoon too is blowing, he thinks.

What's this? Not a soul in sight in this wide open space! Where have they all gone? Is it because of the wind that they haven't turned up?

Open, empty space. There are cows grazing. In the distance lies the graveyard. At the outermost edge, close to the lagoon, stands a solitary coconut tree, its branches swaying.

"Chee," he gives vent to his irritation and disappointment.

He goes back and confines himself to the house. It's dark. The time is seven o'clock when he used to go to the reading room. He thinks of going to the park.

What's this?

The streetlights glow faintly like candles.

The reading room seems lifeless. The light outside is too dim for playing cards. Could that be the reason for the absence of life? Inside, two small boys flicking through magazine pages, looking at pictures.

39

They have school books; perhaps they are returning from tuition classes. Julius's father is going through the paper. Reading tables and empty benches.

He glances at the magazines perfunctorily, unable to concentrate. It wasn't like this before. He leaves.

Subramaniam Park too is deserted . . . An affected voice comes over a radio; seated on the stone benches in front of the radio are the same old cronies indulging in political gossip.

Silence in the background. The bulb at the gate lights up the fountain, the slide, and the tall trees, all partly shrouded in darkness.

This loneliness, the utter absence of human beings . . . he doesn't like it at all now. Before, there was inner satisfaction and pleasure: alone till the news broadcast was over, then walking back and forth on the gravel path in the fading light, was so satisfying.

Loneliness. Does it have any meaning?

Now it seems madness to him. One must move with people. Surely, I'm not the only person in the world; one can no longer be a Robinson Crusoe.

A day has passed. Why hasn't Christurasa come? Oh, but today is Sunday . . . they won't put out to sea.

"Christurasa!"

"He isn't here, Thamby . . . only last week he went to Thalayady. His job is such he has to stay there, it seems," says Christurasa's mother coming out of the house.

"Why does he have to stay there?"

"He has a mason's job now. He doesn't go fishing any longer."

How to pass his leave period without Christurasa? If he had been here, we could have talked at length about books and local affairs, which I enjoy.

Christurasa was his most intimate friend.

Who else?

Only empty space.

St Louis, Alphonsus. Friendship with them was confined only to an exchange of smiles . . . the boys who frequented the reading room had different tastes.

It appears, then, there's no one else.

Ten o'clock in the morning. Time more for midday heat. There's a gathering under the shade tree in front of the reading room. Jacob's tea boutique is filled with boys who have returned from the night's fishing.

Oh, but today they don't put out to sea. That's why they are gathered here. Thevathas crosses and goes past him as if he had not noticed him. Can't he even smile? Why, does he think I'll slight him? Have I changed so much?

Is it my job in Colombo in the Postmasters and Signallers Service? And that too in just one year?

There's an appreciative crowd watching the seafaring boys playing cards.

"I am not important to them. Earlier, I too didn't take any notice of them. So why should they talk to me?"

Faces that don't come close.

Tense and ill at ease, he goes to the reading room. Chee, why did I come back to this place?

Irritated, his mind desiccated by loneliness, he returns home and confines himself to the easy-chair with his books, till nightfall.

Where to go? Whom can I visit?

Including today, it's three days. Five days more to go, he says irritably. If I go to Colombo . . .

Colombo? A vegetarian hotel for his meals, confined to the third bed in the only single room. From Wellawatte to Fort and from Fort to Wellawatte every day, meaninglessly, like a machine.

"What's this? Why are you shutting yourself up in the house, go out, meet friends and talk to them instead of sitting here like a madman thinking all the time?" Amma says, perhaps irritated with him.

"To whom can I talk?"

"Oh, you're a funny person. Why did you come here then?"

WHY DID YOU COME HERE THEN?

These words keep echoing.

Yes, why did I come here? To become dried up?

My mother too asks that question.

Where is Amma? She's not around, she must have gone out.

I must free myself from this state of irritation. It's only 5.30 now. I can leave by this evening mail train.

Hurriedly he packs his clothes drying outside.

Akka too is not around. Perhaps she has gone next door. *Thangachchi* alone is in the house. I mustn't come here for long periods. Have to live somehow in damned Colombo."

As he approaches the entrance, carrying his suitcase, Amma walks in, opening the door.

"Where are you going with the suitcase?" she asks in surprise.

"I'm going to Colombo."

"What is this . . . all of a sudden . . . you have yet some more days of leave." She seems frightened, as if I am going far away from them.

Irritated, he keeps quiet.

Amma cries. "I don't understand . . . why are you angry with us . . . you are not your old self. How much I struggled to educate you."

"What's this? Why are you crying for nothing?"

My words make her think I'm rebuking her.

"You must listen to a mother's words. Why are you leaving like this, all of a sudden. Are you going to forget us all?"

His irritation increases. It's time for the train.

"I don't know . . . I'm going."

He doesn't look back. It's a pretty long walk to the railway station. No one to accompany me.

With his suitcase, He passes under the light at the Beach Road Junction. In the distance the evening shadows lengthen.

Translated by A J Canagaratna

The Cadjan Fence

K V NADARAJAN

The bustle and activity of the day subside as the sun begins to set and darkness spreads throughout the village.

The mother is busy at the fireplace.

Seated near the table, the daughter who is studying asks "Where is Thamby, Amma? How long it's been since the lamp was lit."

"For four or five days he has been pestering me to see a film. You know your father's nature. When he arrives, the boy can't move an inch this way or that. That's why I allowed him to go to a film, Thangachchi. He'll come before ten o'clock. Poor boy, he too has desires like others his age."

"Amma, why are you all the time in the kitchen?"

"How can I disturb your studies? Your appa is very fond of my *thosais*. Where he is he has to manage with restaurant food. That's why I have let the *ulundu* soak. I'm going to grind it now."

A figure goes past the gate whistling "*Singara Vela.*" The daughter knows the tune well.

"My stomach is rumbling. I want to go to the toilet," the daughter says, as if to herself but loud enough for the mother to hear.

"Thangachchi, take the lamp with you."

"My father's coming from Colombo tomorrow. Don't forget yourself and smile at me. Don't go whistling down the lane. *Appa* is very suspicious," the daughter tells her lover in a low voice.

"If he's your father, then he's my father-in-law. I'm going to ask him to give you to me in marriage."

"What cheek! If you dare to ask him, he'll give you the *ekel*- broom treatment. If he finds out I talk to you, he'll kill me . . . you are always up to your pranks . . . your habit while driving of tooting the horn

43

makes you always want to toot and fondle mine."

"You say I shouldn't see you or talk to you when your father comes. Then come soon."

"My mother might come any moment . . . enough, enough."

"I'm going to marry you . . . that's a promise."

"But then you said that you want to study further."

"I'm doing so because Aiya wants me to study. What's the harm in studying?"

"No sign of her yet . . . child, child!" the mother's voice comes from the kitchen.

"Coming, Amma, I'm coming! . . . Please go soon."

The lover climbs back over the fence and disappears.

The fence which has witnessed the lovers' tryst sighs.

"Let's sit here, not in the house. The boy is fast asleep, having seen a film. But the girl keeps on coughing. She is a big girl, no," the mother says, leaning against the protective wall of the well, beside herself in ecstasy.

"If Aiya comes, how long will he be here?"

"He wrote he's coming on a week's leave. That's why I sent word you must definitely come today."

"This year too you must help me to get the lease to tap the trees."

"To whom else will he lease it? Will I allow him to lease it to anyone else? This is my dowry property. Hug me tight."

"Alright, come later . . . the girl keeps on coughing Tomorrow Aiya will be here . . . bring him two bottles of Palmyra toddy at ten in the morning tomorrow. Poor man, he doesn't touch anything in Colombo. Only when he comes here."

"Does Amma have to tell me. Every time Aiya comes it is I who have supplied the toddy."

He climbs back over the fence.

The fence which has witnessed the goings-on of the mistress of the house, sighs again.

Picking up a stick, Aiya beats the fence to dislodge the white ants, saying, "The fence has rotted and is crumbling."

"Yes, Appa . . . the child too is now a big girl. You'll have to make the fence a little higher. Next month the cheetu money will come," the mother says.

The fence which from generation to generation has been the guardian of Jaffna's honour and dignity does not feel cheered by the news that it is going to be raised a foot higher. It merely sighs again, as it sets about performing its traditional role.

Translated by A J Canagaratna

Toil

MURUGAIYAN

In its majestic grandeur
the chariot shines
reaching out
into the blue sky.

The bulls below, yoked to the chariot
exhausted, panting
foaming at the mouth,
the chariot moves as the animals pull.

The glittering wooden horses
prominent above
frozen in galloping postures;
people lose sight of
the tired beasts below.

Translated by the author

Ancient Burdens

MURUGAIYAN

Twenty centuries of ancient baggage
heaped together, slung across
our backs,
we began our long journey.
Fragmented relics, broken and shattered,
torn, tattered and rotten remnants;
all those we gathered together
our backs bent, our eyes narrowed
we began our journey through the world.

Twenty centuries of baggage.

Those without baggage
ambled along empty handed.
They walked without
the journey's burdens
walked without a care.
Others carrying weapons,
fought, conquered
made heaven on earth
shared with all,
not tired they walked together
all this they did
and will do more, they claimed.

Having seen this
we did not even think
to unload our ancient baggage,

rested and refreshed
spread the contents
discard rubbish, retain the gems
and go forth.
We never thought
as fatigue increased
and backs hurt
we crawled, and crawled, and crawled.

As others shrunk their
baggage to fit
their wallets and worked
with bare hands
wrought wonders
with thought and work and will
won victories and shaped the world
we, grown weary
tormented by the load
crawled, crawled, endlessly
crawled.

To sift the unwanted, collect the gems
to move ahead, we do not know
twenty centuries of burden
conflicts in the name of culture.

Translated by Chelva Kanaganayakam

The Naked Wretch

M PONNAMBALAM

He stripped his cloth and wrapped his head
and stood in splendid nakedness.
The passing idlers clapped and jeered
and jeering pelted unkind stones.
Unconcerned, he passed them all;
shots and stones unceasing came
the women cast a sidelong glance,
then feigned a blush and turned away.

An aged one in wonder said,
"This crazy man is full of lust."
Did this wonder strike him too?
He stopped and gazed with upturned eyes
the earth and trees then met his gaze.
My kith and kin the world around
he seemed to say, and then went on.

The cops rushed up and stood aghast,
his deeds perplexed and struck them mute.
They stared and then they bade him dress
he turned away and they went mad.
They swore at him with obscene words
and rained their blows upon his head;

this blessed man then closed his eyes
and naked fell upon the naked earth.

Translated by Chelva Kanaganayakam

Among the Hills

N S M RAMAIAH

Ranjitham walked on wearily. Her face looked flushed in the rising heat. Sweat beaded her forehead, and a few wet strands of hair had escaped the cloth she had tied around her head. Beyond her the tea pickers still swarmed around the place where the tea leaves were being weighed. She was not fully aware that she too had already been there and returned. Her thoughts were fixed on the events of the previous day.

Even now her body seemed to burn as she thought of it. For one year she had awaited this event. She had woven so many dreams in her imagination, and now the very foundation seemed shattered. This was not the first occasion that Ranji's father had said no to those who came with a marriage proposal. On those earlier occasions Ranji was not surprised. In fact, she had sighed with relief. She had felt that the god to whom she prayed had steeled her father's heart to ensure her survival. Now that same god had cheated her.

Between her and Muthiah there had been "something" for about a year. As a result she had resolved never to risk her neck for any man but him. Yesterday it was Muthiah's people who had come asking for a bride and returned empty handed. As she wondered what she would do next, a thought, a memory, still fresh in her mind, bloomed and spread its fragrance.

It was almost noon.

The gravelled road sprinkled over with sand made the air intolerably hot. Ranji was walking rapidly as if to seek shelter in her own shadow. She held a tiffin carrier in each hand, and on her shoulders were slung two bags from which peeped a number of thermos flasks like kangaroos. If the tea-picking took place on a hill far away from the lines, then someone had to go and bring lunch for the kanganies. Today it was her turn.

In the distance Muthiah was seated in the shadow of a casuarina tree sharpening a knife on a log the size of a pestle. The knife, sharpened on granules of fine sand, gleamed like silver. The bushes were being pruned on that hill. The other workers had finished their work and gone. There was no one else around at the time—not even a bird. The whole mountain had taken on the appearance of a closely shaven grey head. In his half-finished section, some unpruned tea bushes still stood with their heads high, like a single row of seedlings in a bare field.

"Whoever did that is bone lazy," thought Ranji to herself.

Muthiah heard the approaching steps and glanced up at Ranji. She was a bit surprised to see that it was indeed Muthiah's section. She knew that he was considered an expert in pruning.

He wiped the beads of sweat from his forehead with his forefinger. A thin stream rolled down. He flicked it off with his thumb a couple of times and said, "Look, you . . . "

Rani was aghast. He was her brother Kandan's friend all right. In fact, he had come home on a few occasions to meet Kandan. She passed him, took a few steps, then paused, half turned, and asked, "What?" The anxiety that lurked in her eyes, like that of a bewildered cat, made him laugh.

"Can you give me a little tea if you have some in there?"

The gentleness of his tone reassured her.

"Really?" she asked with mock scorn. "As if you've been working so hard! Not even half the job is done yet." As she said this she burst out laughing.

"What did you say? Not even half. . . ?"

Neither of them bothered to complete the sentence. Ranji started to walk away.

"Do you know whose portion of work that is?" asked Muthiah, the tone of his voice a shade higher. "Your brother's . . . it's his."

Ranji slowed down, stopped, and then turned around to look at him. His head was bent, and he seemed to be testing the sharpness of the knife.

"This is what happens when you try to do good in this world," he muttered and started whetting his knife.

She felt ashamed. Here was a man asking for a little water to quench his thirst, and she had attacked him like an enraged buffalo. She bit her lips in embarrassment, lowered the tiffin carrier and then pulled out a flask—her own blue flask. Her whole body seemed to tingle as she gently asked, "Do you want some?"

Muthiah lifted his head. For a second there was no one to be seen. He let his eyes roam and then stopped. A single eye was looking at him from behind a tree. Muthiah smiled mischievously. That single eye too disappeared behind the tree. With his hands on his knees, he stood up. As he moved towards her she came out of hiding, picked up the flask, placed it a few feet away from her and then retreated. He lifted the flask opened the lid, and drank at a gulp. In a moment he wrinkled his face.

"Ah, there's no sugar!"

Ranji bit her lower lip to suppress her laugh and then took out a small packet of sugar from her waist. As she opened the packet and took a pinch of sugar he wiped his hand on his waist cloth and stretched it out. A tiny mound of sugar appeared on his palm. He looked at it and said, "Is this how you drink it? We add sugar to the tea."

She tried to look severe. "You are big people. You can do it that way. Can all of us afford to do the same?" Before she could finish, she turned her eyes away bashfully. Her toe scraped the sand, causing a tiny depression.

He licked the sugar, crunched it between his teeth and drank some more tea. A few drops fell on his chin and took a winding path down to his Adam's apple.

As he returned the half-finished flask, she said, "Give that to my brother." She then adjusted the flasks and picked up the tiffin carriers.

"Wait a minute," he said.

Muthiah went back to the spot where he had been seated. He chose the low-hanging branch of the Murunga tree, hung the flask, then sat down under a tea bush and spread out his head cloth. Directly under the bush in the shade lay heaped about three pounds of leaves. These he made into a bundle and gave to Ranji. As he put the bundle down in front of her and opened it, her face, eyes, and lips widened in joy and amazement.

"So much!" she said to herself.

"Take it," he said. "I didn't feel like pruning with the leaves still on, so I kept on picking. I suppose if I wanted to, I could have collected a lot more. Will you take it with the cloth?"

"No."

Her waist bag lay folded above her knees. She dropped all the leaves into the bag. A few glances at him expressed all her gratitude.

The relationship which began thus was now in the balance. As she walked, at a distance, Muthiah's sister Valli lowered her basket to the ground and waited for her to come up. This would be their first encounter following yesterday's incident, and Valli had heaps of things to talk about. She had not been unaware of the "affair." Yesterday's incident had shocked her.

As Ranji came up to Valli, she looked up for a moment, then lowered her eyes and continued walking. Valli kept pace with her. For a while there was a meaningful silence. Valli felt her head would burst if she didn't talk, so she touched Ranji's hand and asked, "What happened?"

Ranji gave a lifeless laugh. They chose a shady spot and sat down. Valli opened a flask, wiped the cup with the end of her sari, poured some tea and held it out to her. Ranji took it.

"Why did your father say that?"

Ranji gazed at the cup and remained silent.

"You are already twenty-five. Is that not enough? How much longer are you going to wait?"

Ranji's eyes grew wet and a flood of tears rolled down her cheeks. She wiped her eyes with the cloth on her head.

"Your father is crazy about money," said Valli with finality. "If he lets you get married then he will lose your salary of eighty or ninety rupees, won't he?"

For a few moments the surge of emotion prevented further words.

"My brother is awfully upset," said Valli.

"Did he say anything?" Ranji's voice trembled.

"No, nothing." Valli, who had been gazing absently at a tea bush now turned and said gently, "He didn't even eat last night." Her voice shook, and Ranji breathed a deep sigh. "I'll tell you something; will you listen?" asked Valli.

Ranji looked up.

"Why don't you simply come home with me?"

Ranji's eyes narrowed.

"Why not? There's no point trusting your father. Even after five years you will still be like this. You come home, and we will look after you like gold."

Ranji felt there was some truth in what Valli said. She looked sharply at Valli for a moment and then lowered her eyes. A thousand thoughts, like the broken fragments of dried mud, came crowding into her head. Should she go?

What was wrong in doing that? In any case, was there an alternative? The face of Muthiah, disappointed, unable to eat, floated into her mind. A blind desire to go with Valli took possession of her.

Valli placed a hand on Ranji's shoulder and said, "Why do you delay? Are you waiting for an auspicious hour?"

Ranji finally came to a decision, she would go. She did not know if it was morally right. She did not know if it was legally right. But she felt she had to do it. She had fought a tremendous battle within herself, and now she longed for comfort. If she was to continue the drudgery of her past life, she might as well soak herself in kerosene and set fire to herself. After all, even her passion was burning her up.

That evening, as she held Valli's hand and stepped into their house, it was like going to the bridal bed to meet her husband. Her heart beat fast. She had been in this house a number of times. But now it was different. They hung their baskets on a nail on the wall of the verandah and stepped into the house.

It was somewhat dark inside the old line house. The house consisted of a verandah with a seat outside and one room. There was only one entrance. There was just one window in the room, with bars across, like in a jail.

Valli's mother was totally engrossed in the cooking. She had draped on a sari without a blouse, revealing half her back and half her stomach.

She sensed that someone had come in and turned. For a moment she was amazed to see Ranji. But as Valli went up to her, knelt down, and explained, her face lit up, and she smiled. She came to Ranji, stroked her cheeks and pressed her fingers on the dot of paste on her forehead.

Valli cracked her knuckles. She was thoroughly elated. She dragged Ranji around to the garden and the water pipe. By the time they had had a wash and returned, Valli's mother was ready with the tea. Even as Ranji drank, she was reminded that at this time her tea at home would be going cold and collecting dust in the white jug. A small child, one of Valli's brothers, appeared. He was naked and stood staring at Ranji with two fingers in his mouth. Ranji drew him to her, held him close, combed back his hair, and said,

"It's not nice to run around like that. Be a good child. Go put some clothes on, will you?" The boy bolted, and all three of them laughed.

Ranji remembered that she too had a brother like this one. She had fed him. He insisted on sleeping by her side. Her heart melted at the thought of him. "Hhow long can a girl stay in her parental home?" she thought to herself.

It was now over half an hour since she had come. Muthiah had not yet returned. She wondered how he would react upon seeing her. What she imagined was certainly comforting. However a part of her heart had grown dark and from within the gloom came four or five crying voices. The memory of her brothers and sisters, who were her responsibility, obsessed her. Her family was large. From the earnings of three, nine of them had to survive. It had been a struggle in the past. How would it be for them now?

Her mother was totally incapable of looking after the children. If their mischief became intolerable, she would merely slap her head a couple of times and scream, "Don't kill me you devils!" and start weeping. Weakened by repeated childbirths, she too was like a child to Ranji. As she thought of her now, the idea of shifting her burden on to another brought a pang of conscience. Her mother, who would enroll for work only on those rare days when she felt well, would now be forced to work every day. It was difficult and painful to think of her dark, emaciated mother going daily to work.

Outside, the twilight dimmed, and darkness set in. Leaving Ranji alone, Valli went in and brought two lanterns, polished the chimneys, then poured some kerosene and lit them. Valli's mother had finished her cooking and gone to visit her neighbor. For a long time Ranji sat still and then quietly stood up and came close to Valli. Her eyes were moist, and her lips trembled. She said gently, "Valli." Even that word sounded like a sob. She wiped her nose with the edge of her sari.

As Valli looked up, it was obvious to her that Ranji had been crying for some time.

"What is it?" she asked.

"I'm going home."

"What?"

Ranji wiped her face and nose once more. Valli stood up, shook Ranji's shoulders, and asked, "What has come over you?"

Ranji calmly went to the clothes line, pulled off her cloth and sack, and returned to the verandah. Valli, who had been following her, held her hand and said, "Ranji, where are you going? Come inside."

Ranji's eyes were now red with crying. "No, Valli, let me go home." She slipped out of Valli's hold. "It's not right, my coming like this. Do you think the earnings of my father and brother are enough for my family?" Even as she said this she felt the tears welling up within her. "I can't bear to leave the little ones alone." She broke down and sobbed. Valli hardly knew what to say.

The basket was taken off the nail. Ranji put the cloth sack into it, placed the rope over her head and stepped out. She did not speak to or even look at Valli, who stood absolutely still, too stunned even to call her mother.

Ranji merged with the darkness and began to run.

Translated by Chelva Kanaganayakam

Tea Baskets

KASTURI

On greedy scales
baskets of tea;
the bushes
yearn for tea
when will they rise
to burn their torments?

Translated by Chelva Kanaganayakam

Self-rule

M PONNAMBALAM

The shadowless Southern temple
stands erect
its shadow turned inward
it towers above.
Gaze at me, not my shadow
seek refuge in me, not my shadow
my gaze is myself
my refuge is myself.

A long shadow of art befalls life.
In shadows of art
admiration and refuge
not in life.
No art in life, no beauty in art
both beauty and life
to see and love himself
man seeks shadows.

When human actions cast no shadow
and rise majestic
like the Southern temple
the shadow of art in beauty
destroys itself,
sheds light on life.
Now
life itself is art
and the shadow
seeks a closure
ends the book of art, opens life.

Translated by Chelva Kanaganayakam

The Strike

K SADDANATHAN

For two days he had been unable to do anything. He seemed to have lost his balance; his agitation prevented him from concentrating on anything. He had the feeling that his inner wholeness has slipped out of him. Today he had gone to work and returned. Could he go tomorrow? He felt frightened.

After his return from work each day, he had confined himself to the house, without even bothering to wash his face at the well. In one way, this provided him some security.

This sudden withdrawal surprised and embarrassed him. It was only the day before yesterday they had taken this decision on behalf of their Union. The parent Union too had instructed them to participate in the General Strike.

A section of the Railway had already struck. They had received information that, following that example, government clerical servants and other trade unions had also gone on strike.

After all this, could they keep quiet? They called a committee to discuss the situation. Only eight members turned up for the committee meeting. He too had taken part in it in his capacity as secretary of the organization.

All had behaved very circumspectly, without betraying their hand. However, one or two voices had raised a feeble protest.

"Why can't we go on striking after drawing this month's salary?"

"I'm on extension. I can't strike."

"Why not postpone a decision on this matter?"

"If the job goes, it's gone forever . . . are these chaps going to give it back to us?"

"Siva, Theva, Thiagu, Kunam, Dias—only they will go on strike."

At the end of the meeting, without any firm decision being taken, they had chatted with one another and dispersed.

That July 22 was an appropriate day was the only thing imprinted on their memory.

When he woke up, it was past five pm. He wanted to remain inside the house as far as possible. He thought it dangerous even to go out.

He knew that if he went out, the very first person he encountered would drag him into a discussion about the strike.

The way they talked, as if he had nothing else but the strike as a talking point, irritated and bored him.

After washing his face at the well, he took the cup of tea from his younger sister.

"Does Indu, like anna, go on strike?" he asked her.

"What is this, Anna? What is there to mope about in this?

She took the empty tumbler and went inside.

It seemed as if there was no one with whom he could discuss the subject frankly and intimately.

In the morning, his father's mocking look had grieved him. Now the younger sister had dismissed him in a few words.

Mother seemed somewhat upset. But her anxiety lacked insight and understanding.

Just then he remembered Chandra. He felt that he should see her.

He had met Chandra only six months earlier. He had gone to the Kachcheri to see about a registration in the Land Registry Office. When he was returning, his mission unaccomplished, it was Chandra who had come to his help.

He was completely surprised when she was able to finalize the matter in ten minutes.

The mere thought that he had wasted four days trying to accomplish his task completely embarrassed him.

It was his nature to be withdrawn, not to take the initiative in anything. Her bustling, active nature appealed to him.

He looked shyly at Chandra.

"How is Indu?" she asked him.

"Do you know Indu?"

"Of course. I know Indu's anna too."

He smiled.

She smiled too.

They met each other frequently without sullying the innocence of that smile. They talked and smiled fondly.

Once she invited him to her home. Though he was a little reluctant at first, he accepted her invitation and spent some time with her.

When he went in search of her, she was alone in the house, writing something. She came out and invited him to her room.

The room was orderly; it seemed to him that this was her study. The walls were colour-washed a very light blue. There was a sofa near the window, perhaps to relax and lie down while reading.

Her table was along the eastern wall. Above the beautiful table lamp, there was a picture of the turbaned Bharati on the wall. On the left of the room were two shelves full of books.

He was happy to note that she was a reader. He himself was a voracious reader.

The manuscripts lying on the table indicated that she was not only a reader but a writer too.

"What is all this writing about trade union matters? Do you participate in that too?"

"Why not?" she said with a smile and handed him a book from the table. "Here read this, I 'll be back in a minute." She went inside.

When she came out with a cup of coffee in her hands, she noticed he was engrossed in the book.

"Latin American writings are not available here. Can I give it back after finishing it?"

"Books can't be lent."

"Even to me?"

"What's so special about you?"

His face darkened as he closed the book and silently placed it on the table.

What's this touch-me-not nature; she thought to herself as she picked up the book, placed it in his hands, and said "Give it back after you finish reading it."

The smile playing on her lips touched him. He straightened up and looked at her intently.

This girl with the silken glance is somewhat dark. Her body is slim and supple. She looks as if she has been sculpted. I seem to remember seeing someone like her somewhere.

When he realized what she reminded him of, he was thrilled: the Amman statue in the local temple.

"Finished?"

"What?"

"I asked if you have finished looking."

"At what?"

"At this girl. What is there to be fascinated by in this inky blackness? Enough of looking. Say something."

"Looking is enough."

"What's all this silly sentimentality?"

"What about you?"

Her lips quivered. With his fingers he firmly pressed her lips.

She liked his moderation and balance, which saw to it that he did not overstep the limits, even under pressure of passion.

That day's meeting not only helped them to develop a fondness for each other but also enabled them to understand each other and exchange views on many matters. Common interests and tastes brought them closer to each other. However, there was also something in him which made him withdrawn and turn inward, she noticed. This did not seem an insurmountable barrier to her, caught as she was in the coils of love. She thought that living with him and time would set matters straight.

They talked for a long time and parted reluctantly that day.

Putting on his shirt, he set out to meet Chandra

As he stopped on the road, Sivarasa appeared before him, with a slight smile.

"Machchan, don't forget the twenty-second . . . or else we will be labeled blacklegs."

He felt like breaking the crooked tooth Sivarasa displayed when he smiled and depositing it in his hand.

Sivarasa seemed to be going somewhere in a hurry. Machchan was thankful Sivarasa didn't pursue the matter of the strike.

Hmm . . . how can one run a trade union with weaklings like this . . . ? It's better to give up all this mad work and mind one's own business.

Was it to get trapped like this he had stopped everyone he met on the way and lectured them on socialism?

With a heavy heart, he turned into the mill land. There was a Vairavar Kovil on the lane's eastward bend. He approached the kovil, touched the sulam and worshipped it.

His tongue was dry; something seemed to form in the throat and his eyes became moist.

He circumambulated the withered margosa tree and the sulam thrice. He made a vow that in Chithirai he would perform a pongal.

How many vows he had made to this Vairavar; the vow he had made when he had touched the arichchuvadi with tiny fingers and asked for the boon of learning, the vow made when Amma had fallen seriously ill and was fighting for her life, the vows made when he had passed the exam, got a job, fallen in love with Chandra . . .

Why all these vows and pongals . . . ? He felt ashamed when he recalled them.

When, with a measured walk, he turned at the culvert, he saw Chandra's house.

Chandra was at home. Her sympathetic and cordial welcome gave him strength. He felt he had come to the right place. Though he was eager to unburden his mind, he hesitated not knowing where to begin.

It was Chandra who spoke first.

"Aren't you on strike tomorrow?"

Not wanting to answer her directly, he came close to her and, holding her hands in his, said: "It's better to forget all this madness and go to work instead."

She felt something inside her snap and bleed.

Such a bundle of contradictions, she thought as her face darkened and set hard.

"Aren't you ashamed to talk like this?" she asked sharply.

Can I betray my helplessness to a person like her who acts so decisively? he thought as he looked at her in silence.

Her look seemed to say, How can I have any relationship or intimacy with someone who begins to quake in fear over a small matter such as this?

"Is this a small matter?"

"For girl-like people, it's a big matter. Go well in time to school to-morrow. Go and sign the attendance register."

Her words unsettled him utterly. It seemed to him that the Chandra who had been so close to him had gone far, far away from him, that he had been swept to a side. He began to sweat all over his body. He came out fearing even to look at her and took his leave. He didn't feel like returning home; he went where his legs took him. Walking wasn't difficult for him; it relaxed him. He walked a long distance, not taking notice of anything. He thought the sound of the sea came from Cheddipulam. A mosque could be seen in the distance. Leaping tongues of flame. The smell of a human body burning. He realized he was standing near the madam of a crematorium. He looked hard at the burning corpse without any sense of fear. In the midst of the tongues of flame, leaping from the pyre was Chandra. Her burning corpse seemed to smile mockingly at him. Startled, he left the crematorium. He walked fast up to the matha kovil; then fearing to take the short cut through Chatti, he began to walk along the road.

He thought his senses had become dulled after he parted from Chandra.

When he reached home it was past ten pm.

He pretended to eat something, to satisfy his mother, then withdrew once more to his room.

Chandra's nature is to view and do everything as a matter of course . . . Her parents depend on her, her earnings . . . But why am I unable to do what she can? Appa's wholesale rice business is unable to fortify me and give me courage. Is this lack of courage a manifestation of my weakness, of my instinct for self-preservation, as Chandra says? Will her oft-repeated statement "You'll get Chandra only if you get rid of this middle-class mentality" come true?

He felt frightened. He felt as if he should tear his hair. Tears came to his eyes. Biting his lips, he got up, opened the window and looked out. The unobscured moon shone brightly,

Will Chandra be asleep now? Not likely. She might be reading something.

He was troubled by the feeling that something which had been very close to him had dissolved and flowed away.

He came out of his room. His mother was sleeping on the bare cement floor in the hall. Poor Amma, he thought as he went back to bed.

When he went to school in the morning, he found that the principal had arrived before him. After signing the attendance register, he went to the chemistry lab and secluded himself there. He decided that as far as possible he would hold classes in his lab.

Pandithar, Thangarasa, Samby, SK, VS Shan—all seemed to peep at him and smile derisively as they went past.

Only Vanitha came into the lab, remarked sympathetically, "You haven't gone on strike. That's good," and left.

Why can't Chandra be like Vanitha? he thought for a moment.

He had wanted to see Chandra before he came to school in the morning. But he had changed his mind. It seemed absurd to him to continue to talk to Chandra on this matter. It appeared to him that she was bent on damaging his ego, whatever the topic of conversation was.

Wasn't it my mistake to talk of love to a clever, resourceful girl like her, he wondered now and then.

It surprised him that his mind was dissolving in memories about her.

As soon as school ended, he hurriedly caught the bus, not wishing to meet even his colleagues.

He had taken just a few steps, having alighted from the bus, when he saw Chandra. He hadn't expected to see her; he froze. She pretended not to see him or notice his feelings. Walking fast, she passed him. He watched her walking away. At that moment, the thought of Vanitha came to his mind. The sympathy exuding from her wide eyes was always consoling.

When he reached home, Indu came running and said, "Chandra came, Anna."

He was unable to say anything. He looked up at his sister. Her eyes were moist.

"Chandra is on strike, why don't you go on strike at least tomorrow?"

"Go on strike! For whose sake, Vanitha's?"

"What is this, 'for Vanitha?' "

"No, I asked whether it was for Chandra's sake?"

Indu stared at him as if she understood.

At that moment he thought Vanitha's eyes were more beautiful than Chandra's.

Translated by A J Canagaratna

The Dematagoda Refugee

A SANTHAN

He looked up when he heard someone unlatching the gate. A woman, an unknown person, walked in briskly with a child on her shoulder. As she came closer, he was sure he hadn't seen her before.

When she approached the verandah, he got up and asked her politely, "Who do you wish to see?"

Moving closer to him, she put the child on the step of the verandah and said, "I have come from the other side of the Amman temple . . . " Her eyes glistened with tears.

He was disturbed.

"We were at Dematagoda during the riots last year . . . ," she said, her voice trembling.

Moved by her grief, he went inside and called his mother: "Amma."

"He was killed then . . . ," the woman continued, when he returned.

"Who?"

"His father," she said, pointing to the child.

The child stared at him. Those lovely eyes made the child's face very attractive. "He must be less than five years," he thought. He felt an urge to take the child in his arms, and he smiled at the thought. The child, scared, hid behind his mother.

His mother came out, calling, "Enna?"

The woman repeated her story.

"Aiyo!" exclaimed his mother, once the woman had finished, "How awful!"

She called the woman in and asked her to sit down.

This was their village, said the woman. Her grandfather was a man from the area. But they had been away twenty years or so. They didn't have a house here but owned only a plot of land, near Ambalam master's house. No, master was not a relative of theirs, but knew them well. If you inquire from him, he'll tell you everything. She intended to put up a hut for herself and her child in their plot, but she had no money.

His mother, who was listening intently, turned away when the woman had finished. He noticed his mother wiping her eyes with the border of her saree as the woman walked in.

"Where were you staying at Dematagoda?" he asked more for the sake of conversation than anything else.

"Along the road to Wellawatte."

"What? Were you in the refugee camp?"

"Yes."

"Where? Which camp?"

"At Veyangoda."

"Really!"

The child came and looked at him with a smile.

His mother returned and called the woman. The woman went up to her.

"Keep this," said his mother, handing her something.

The woman took it, brought both her palms together and bowed to his mother. Then, placing the child on her waist, she thanked his mother again and left.

He watched the woman walking towards the gate and stepping down the road. Then, turning to his mother, he asked irritably:

"Why did you give her that? All that she told you were blatant lies."

He told her about the woman's story.

"Don't be a fool," snapped his mother, "do you expect a woman like her to know the geography of the big city where she lived? She must be very naïve," she declared.

He wished it were so.

Translated by S Rajasingam

Your Fate Too

JESURASA

You stroll back home
from the beach
or maybe from the cinema.
Suddenly a rifle cracks
boots scamper away.
You'll lie dead
on the road.
In your hand
a dagger sprouts
a pistol too may blossom.
"A terrorist,"
you'll be dubbed.
No one
dare ask questions.
Silence freezes.
But
deep in the people's minds
indignation bubbles up.

Translated by A J Canagaratna

Exile Days

P AKILAN

Good Friday
The day they crucified you.

A hot wind
blew between shore and sea.
One or two sea crows
flew in the immaculate sky.
The wind grating the palymrah trees
whipped up inexpressible horror
That was the last day in our village.
We came ashore
only the waves returned.
When the sun fell into the sea
we knelt down and wept.
An eerie howl rose
became night.
In the distance
like a single corpse in the cemetery
burnt our village.

Good Friday
the day they crucified you.

Translated by S Canagarajah

Murder

M A NUHMAN

Last night
I dreamt
Buddha was shot dead
by the police,
guardians of the law.
His body drenched in blood
on the steps
of the Jaffna library!*

Under cover of darkness
came the ministers.
"His name is not on our list,
why did you kill him?"
they ask angrily.

"No sirs, no,
there was no mistake.
Without killing him
it was impossible
to harm even a fly—
Therefore . . . ," they stammered.

"Alright, then
hide the corpse."
The ministers return.

The men in civies
dragged the corpse

into the library.
They heaped the books
ninety thousand in all,
and lit the pyre
with the Cikalokavadda Sutta.
Thus the remains
of the Compassionate One
were burned to ashes
along with the Dhammapada.

* The Jaffna Public Library was burned down in an incident of ethnic violence.

Translated by S Pathmanathan

New Lanka

SOLAIKKILI

Says who?
Speak.
Armstrong has not stepped on the moon.

If in ´86
he claims that science rules the roost
fill his mouth with sand
stitch his mouth across
tell the clown to shut up.

You!
Believe me, fool
manmade moons are not afloat
test-tube babies do not kiss;
still believing that blood is
green and red;
anyone who says that stones
were brought from the moon
slipper him.

Listen!
research underwater is a blatant lie,
if checking a fetus
for a penis
is possible

Where did these Ravanas appear from?
Faces disfigured like demons

SOLAIKKILI

inspiring fear
betrayers of humanity
mutating giants
from where did these legions appear?

Not what you think
hardly a new world
the Lanka torched by Hanuman

Go look
Sita may still be in prison.

Note: This poem is a response to the ethnic clashes in Kalmunai, 10 August, 1986.

Translated by Chelva Kanaganayakam

Trees

S SIVASEGARAM

You step on grass
short shrubs you kick and trample.
Trees, tall and erect, refuse to bow.
Axe in hand you cut them down.

Fools, you do not know
the wonder of trees
springing up from root and seed.

The day your weapon weighs you down
and metal yields to make a rope
to bind your hands and wring your neck
fallen trees will rise
in a forest around you.

Translated by the author

The Gutter of Peace

SHANMUGAM SIVALINGAM

Seated for days on end
Thamil doves and Muslim doves
defecate in the gutter of peace.

Clattering in the sky above
a black Indo-Lankan dragonfly
will visit every day.

The cinder and ashes of Kaaraithievu
are replicated in Maalihaikkaadu—
with one difference:
the mosques of Maalihaikkaadu
do not have statues to knock off.

Indian soldiers sit up
behind stacked-up bags of sand
at every junction
of abandoned streets void of people.

Here and there
on either side
kidnappings until sunset,
on either side
burials at sunset.

Amidst this,
seated for days on end
Thamil doves and Muslim doves
defecate in the gutter of peace.

Translated by A J Canagaratna

Stare at the Sky

KI PI ARAVINDAN

To return home
as dusk falls,
to light a lamp
in a dark house
to eat a morsel
crawl into a corner
to sigh with relief
this is home.

Will these too
now disappear?

Blowing out the lamp
burying in the earth
staring at emptiness
seeking refuge
in the cross
mere phantoms.

Will the city also
die?

The stench of
burnt foliage,
the cry of the helpless
whimpering of dogs;
foaming and panting,
the calf

dodges the noose.

Water dripping from
the roof
the school
the church
everywhere
heaps of scattered dreams.
Humanity in its
collective grief.

The heart gains strength.

Life may slip
in a fraction
At least that would remain.

Stare at the sky.

Translated by Chelva Kanaganayakam

On a Wet Day

SOLAIKKILI

Full bellied
the sky sleeps
a woman, bent over
walks on four legs
rain
bald heads break
nuts fall from trees
rain
trees shed their flowers.

Lightning surveys the land
from a corner of the sea
thunder splits the sky.
The little chick hatched yesterday
dies of shock;
the mother screeches with grief.

I think of paper boats
a wet dog runs ahead
the ash on its back
turns liquid.
Insane,
a fool
to be dreaming
the wind blows leaves on my face
and mother closes the window.

These are memories of rainy days

memories recalled
when hens scratch the yard
and the sky sniffles like a child
bring me the rattle and the soother
to stop the crying child.

Translated by Chelva Kanaganayakam

Butterflies

A MUTTULINGAM

He was refused the visa a second time. He was really frustrated. He couldn't understand the rationale behind it, for hadn't he perfected the forms with the utmost care? Yet, he was refused.

When he had applied the first time, he was truthful. There wasn't any hassle then in obtaining a visa as of now. He was under the impression that the moment you submitted the completed forms, you'd be issued with a visa at once, almost on a plate, as it were.

But in his case something had gone wrong. To the question, "What is the purpose of your visit?" he had responded, "To look at butterflies." That's perhaps where the trouble lay! The officials who studied his application were annoyed at first; then they thought him crazy, treated the whole thing as a big joke and refused him the visa.

When he applied a second time, ten years later, he avoided the word "butterfly" like the plague.

Instead, he said he was going on a holiday and would also drop in at his nephew's place. At the interview he answered the official on the other side of the glass-paneled cubicle with due deference. He also submitted photocopies of his bank balance (of course, he had to borrow the money to inflate his account) and the title deed of his house, to no avail. The heartless officials refused him again.

Some of his friends were of the view that his colleague, Chitrasenan, who taught mathematics in the 'B' division, may have had a hand in the matter. Chitrasenan was notorious for writing anonymous petitions A wheedler par excellence, he had destroyed many a home. They couldn't fathom why he had considered Koneswaran his prime enemy. They were sure Chitrasenan was the culprit and advised Koneswaran to appeal.

Koneswaran refused. He was by nature timid. Moreover, he didn't wish to get into the bad books of the officials at the embassy. He preferred to be patient.

Koneswaran had forgotten that there was a computer in the American Embassy. The information he had given in his first application was safely stored in it. The computer, like an astrologer, compared the information given in the second application with that of the first and found they did not match. His request for a visa was refused.

Though thwarted, he was determined to apply again. This time he did not hide his real intention—he wanted to study a rare breed of butterflies that were to be seen only in the States. He submitted the research articles he had written over the years along with letters from an American professor. This time the officials relented. Who else would persist in applying for a visa over a period of twenty years unless he was genuinely interested in the subject!! He was informed that he would be issued with a visa.

Koneswaran's real vocation was teaching. He taught Advanced Mathematics. His students fondly called him "Cos Theta." Koneswaran. He had thirty students in his class, all geniuses. They would listen to his lectures with rapt attention. Whether they understood him or not was a well-kept secret!

Only the previous day, he had delivered a lecture on the function "sine theta." When he questioned them the next day, they stared at him, their faces blank. He repeated the lesson and then went on to explain the intricacies of "cos theta". The lesson was half-way through when an amazing incident took place.

A butterfly of rare beauty, of a colour the like of which he had never seen before, flew directly into his classroom, like a child breaking free from the loving embrace of its mother, performed a wonderful dance, and flew away through the window.

Koneswaran walked out of the classroom like a man walking in his sleep, a piece of chalk in one hand and a duster in the other. He did not return to the class that day. The lesson on cos theta was left unfinished.

The rumour about this incident spread throughout the school. The principal asked for an explanation. He was a very strict man. Others feared the outcome. Koneswaran was not intimidated. Instead, he not only described to him the beauty of the butterfly but also asked him for two days' leave to capture it. From that day onwards the head's respect for Koneswaran increased. This is how plain Koneswaran became "Cos Theta" Koneswaran.

He was a lover of nature. Simple everyday things sent him into raptures. He never stopped marveling at nature's wonders.

It was said that when he was a child, his mother used to show him butterflies while she fed him. Such was his fascination for butterflies. At the age of three he started chasing and playing with them. By eight he had learnt to catch and mount them. By twenty he had a collection of over a thousand butterflies, preserved and classified scientifically.

Koneswaran was much respected in his village. Though not exactly handsome, he was presentable, nevertheless. His only flaw was his love of and fascination for butterflies. Otherwise, he was naive. A number of local worthies were determined to have him as their son-in-law.

Yamini's father was quite well-off. He was a great lover of Thamil. As if to prove this, he had named his daughter Yamini, "the one born at night." Not only did he give her a formal education but also had her well-schooled in domestic science, music, dress-making and all other social graces required of a future bride. The girl, too, read the local weeklies and the monthly novels assiduously and looked forward to her wedding day.

Though Koneswaran was an expert on butterflies, he was a simpleton when it came to everyday matters. Consider for example what happened on his wedding day. It was customary, as part of the ritual, for the officiating priest to drop a ring into a pot of water and have the couple retrieve it. In reality, it was an occasion for the new couple to feel each other's hands. Even a child of three was aware of this ruse. But not Koneswaran. When Yamini tried to feel his hand, he withdrew it hastily and held out the ring. Poor Yamini, she felt cheated.

The early days of their marriage were a surprise to Yamini. She wondered if there could be any other person who was so enamored of butterflies. The house was full of books and specimens. But she was undaunted. She was determined to win him over soon, one way or another.

Koneswaran had just caught an exotic butterfly and had spent two full days in trying to trace its genealogy but without success. He did not realize that the key to the problem lay with his wife.

It was past midnight. Koneswaran was still engrossed in his work. Yamini did not sleep. She waited for him eagerly. Finally, he closed his books and returned to the bedroom. A great surprise awaited him.

Yamini, like a ripe karutthakolumbaan mango, awaited him in all her splendour. Dressed in a yellow sari, with a big vermilion pottu on her forehead and her luxuriant black hair spread out like dark clouds, she was extremely desirable. When she saw him, she ran towards him with outstretched arms like a kathakali dancer.

Suddenly something struck him. He remembered having read about a butterfly from Thailand that was yellow, vermilion and black in colour. Leaving everything behind, he ran towards his almirah.

It was three am when he returned to bed, flushed with happiness like a child who had found the answer to a riddle. Yamini was fast asleep, her yellow sari in disarray. Koneswaran did not realize to the last the cruelty he had committed that night.

Though fifty, Koneswaran behaved like a child when he obtained the visa. Yamini felt uneasy. He had squandered a lot of money traveling to India and Africa in connection with his research. She didn't mind it then. But America, a far-off place! No, never! But on the other hand, she didn't want to dampen her husband's enthusiasm. After all, hadn't he struggled so long to get this visa?

If getting a visa was a problem, a far greater problem was getting ready to travel to the United States. He had to be there before the end of winter if he wanted to see the monarch butterflies. Wasn't it for this he had persevered for so long?

He managed to get hold of a pair of gloves, a few pairs of woolen socks and a muffler. But what was he to do for an overcoat? He was stuck! Then at a friend's suggestion he went to an old gentleman and asked him to loan him an overcoat if he had one. The gentleman obliged. It had a musty smell. When he tried it on he found it a few sizes too big. He presumed some wrestler like King Kong must have worn it once. "Beggars cannot be choosers," he reasoned and accepted it with alacrity.

It was not unusual for the evil one to manifest itself wherever Koneswaran traveled. Here, in the plane, it was seated beside him. The seat next to his by the window was occupied by a woman of immense size. Her ample breasts completely blocked out the external view. She wore a colored kerchief. Her household goods lay scattered about the place. Like one who had permanently moved out of hearth and home, she sat there snugly, like a chieftain lording over the place, her arms and legs wide apart.

Koneswaran sat down beside her in a fetuslike position. Golden-haired air hostesses floated up and down the plane. Koneswaran's mind, too, did likewise. "Only a couple of hours more," he muttered to himself.

He did not have any problems at Immigration. He answered the official's questions satisfactorily like a three-year-old child repeating the multiplication tables. However, the official could not help looking at this gentleman who had come to see their butterflies with a certain amount of curiosity. Finally, the official stapled the immigration card to the last page of the passport and returned it to him.

He had one more hurdle to clear—Customs. Like all Customs officials elsewhere, this one too appeared stern. It may have been ages since he last smiled. He questioned him closely, dug deep into his suitcase and pulled out a specimen. It was that of a butterfly from New Guinea named "Heaven." He told the official that he was a lepidopterist and had brought the specimen to illustrate his lectures. He begged the official to return it. But the latter did not heed him. Instead he picked it up as he would an earthworm and dropped it into the wastepaper basket. Koneswaran was aghast.

Ganesan waited at the arrivals lounge of San Francisco Airport with some concern. Yamini had written him a twenty page letter describing Koneswaran's physical appearance so that he could identify him easily. But Ganesan had not bargained for what he saw. A Charlie Chaplain-like figure attired in a bulky overcoat, hat and muffler came hurrying towards him awkwardly.

The moment Ganesan recognized him, Koneswaran felt easy. Though he had traveled continuously for twenty hours he looked fresh and sprightly. He was happy because he was soon going to see the monarch butterflies. Meanwhile Ganesan was wandering about the airport car park looking for his car. He had forgotten where he had parked it.

"Thamby, these monarch butterflies travel three thousand kilometres from Alaska to California. They spend the winter here living on the leaves of the milkweed trees. At the beginning of spring they fly back to Alaska, another three thousand kilometres. There they raise their families and at the end of autumn they begin their annual migration to California. This is repeated year in, year out to clockwork precision. Don't you think it remarkable? Can you believe they return to the same tree, the same branch! But here, we have forgotten where we had parked our car a few moments ago."

Ganesan looked at this strange man with awe. For hadn't he traveled over ten thousand miles just to see a butterfly? He must be a crank or a genius!

The next day they motored sixty miles south of San Francisco to the butterfly sanctuary Nature Bridge. The six thousand odd butterflies he had collected over the years paled into insignificance beside a single monarch butterfly! After all, wasn't it the lord and monarch of all other butterflies?

When he looked up, he could see nothing at first . Then he realized that the trees were swarmed with countless red and black monarch butterflies . Who would have imagined so many of them in just one place? Surely this place was holy!

A shudder ran through his entire frame. He couldn't contain the immense joy he felt. His eyes brimmed with tears. He sat there gazing at them, lost in their beauty.

He called Ganesan and held his hands. The latter gently walked him to a wooden bench and sat him there. A couple of passersby stared at them with interest. Ganesan felt ashamed.

Koneswaran was panting. "Thamby, this is a holy place. It is blasphemy for us even to be standing here in our shoes. Haven't I traveled ten thousand miles to see these butterflies? What beauty! Are you aware of the sufferings, shame, indignities and hardships I went through to see these magnificent creatures? I'm prepared to take another birth to see such beauty," he said, sobbing.

"Uncle, just wait a minute. I'll get you a Coke," said Ganesan and went off to buy one. In reality, he was ashamed to be seen with his uncle.

"The troubles I went through to get this visa, the taunts I endured, the number of years I had to wait! But these butterflies fly all the way from Alaska to California. Who demands a visa of them? Hasn't man the freedom these butterflies enjoy? Who issued a visa to Columbus and Vasco da Gama? Did they open out the world only to be hedged in by rules and regulations? What cruelty to demand a visa from those who want to see the splendours of nature? The Himalayas, the Sahara, the Niagara Falls and the Amazon jungle are Nature's gifts to the human. To deny him a visit to these wonders is a crime against humanity.

He sat there looking at them, lost in their beauty, when a wonderful thing happened. A butterfly from one of the topmost trees fluttered towards him, planted a kiss on his left eyebrow and disappeared.

Koneswaran was in ecstasy. Ah, what a soft caress? It came looking for me, me alone and kissed me! Aiyo, did this proud butterfly come in search of me? He was full of tender emotion.

Ganesan approached him with a can of Coke and found him in a state of extreme happiness, his clothes drenched in sweat despite the cold.

Koneswaran took a mouthful of the drink. Then turning to his nephew he said, "Thamby, one needs a visa to travel to the 180 odd nations. But there is one place which doesn't require a visa. Do you know what that place is?"

Ganesan looked at him without replying. Koneswaran lifted his hands and pointed skywards. "One needn't bother about getting a visa to go there. To that extent it's a blessing."

Though it was only four in the evening, darkness soon set in. Since this was winter, the sun too appeared to be in a hurry. Koneswaran woke up from his trance.

"Uncle, shall we return? You've come all the way to see these butterflies. Are you going to return home empty handed without acquiring even a single butterfly for your collection?" asked Ganesan.

Koneswaran replied after some deliberation. "Thamby, I have a collection of almost all kinds of butterflies to be found in the world. This is their lord and sovereign, their monarch. How can I catch it?

Can I do that in a holy place? It would be an act of sacrilege. No, my collection will be complete only if I leave it alone, free." He got up to his feet unsteadily.

He was reluctant to leave the place. Ganesan, however, gently guided him to his car and helped him in. As he was getting in, he was reminded of Sant Nandanar. Koneswaran wondered how Nandanar* would have felt when he had the Lord's dharshan. Again he shuddered.

The car speeded along the highway. Koneswaran slept peacefully, like a well-fed new-born puppy. The seat belt across his bulky over-coat held him securely. His hands and legs were spread out awkwardly.

Ganesan felt uneasy. The deathly silence in the car disturbed him. His words when he spoke were drowned in the howling wind.

"Uncle, have you got all your slides ready for tomorrow's lecture?"

No answer.

"Uncle! Uncle!"

Silence.

Ganesan continued calling him, unaware that his uncle had gone to that land where no visa was required.

---

*Nandanar was an Untouchable. The priests of Chidambaram refused to al-low him into the temple. Lord Shiva, however, gave his devotee darshan out-side the temple.

Translated by S Rajasingam

A Night in Frankfurt

V I S JAYAPALAN

A room in the meanest quarter of Frankfurt.
Crammed like the womb of an impregnated sow.
Like Egyptian mummies
swathed in blankets
lie a pack of helpless Jaffnese.

Wandering mongrel
dog-tired, prone in bed,
scavenging for a living
his days crawl.

The mercury in the stem
contracts to below zero.
A cry rings out in the stillness of night.
Sisters wait, fondly—
with expectations and dreams.
He, a mortgaged title deed
trapped in the village VIP's chest
orphaned in his native land.
A refugee in foreign lands
his youthful life wracked
like storm-stricken Batticaloa.
A something rankles
like a nightmare.
Beside his bedstead
saucepans lie strewn.
Grim reminder of a home
he'll never have.

In his hands, crumpled,
news of a betrayal.
Abandoned,
without home or hearth
a wretch,
he weeps silently
with the snowy evening.

Translated by S Rajasingam

Kosalai

RANJAKUMAR

"Kulam, give the cows some straw, sonny."

Kulam lay on his back on an *ola* mat. He would go to sleep without a pillow. Would his back ache or not? Why was he like a denizen of the jungle?

"The cows are mooing, *appan* . . . give them a little straw," Amma kept on repeating. She was sitting on the *thinnaikkunthu*, her legs outstretched.

Kulam lay jiggling his legs, his elbows firmly pressing his forehead. Amma sat gazing at him: he is of the age when hair sprouts on the chest, the physique of a person becomes prone to violence. His voice too is rough, like his father's. She looked at the hands he had placed on his forehead: the veins stood out prominently. The palms were rough and coarse, like a crocodile's back. The fingers, stained with oil and grease, were dark brown in colour. The tips of the fingers and the nails were stained black with oil.

"Kulam, a little straw."

The son angrily interrupted "You do it . . . I'm tired out."

Amma's smile was tinged with sadness. If Seelan were here, would things have come to this? Without her prodding, he would do all the work. He would feed the cows with straw at the proper times and give them water to drink. He would see to it that the fowls were attended to and shut up in their cages. If occasion arose, he would even scrape coconut for his mother.

What a wonderful son!

Why did he go away like that?

Separated from the village, the fields lay spread out in the distance. In between them were palmyra groves and uplands. In the evenings, Amma would go to the fields to cut and gather grass. It was not possible to ride a bicycle in there. Seelan would wait by the roadside resting against his bicycle. He knew well the times when his mother would come with the bundles of grass. When Amma's figure dimly appeared in the distance, he would leave the road and hurry towards her. He would take over the bundles of grass and fly home on his bicycle, reaching there well before his mother.

On the way back home, Amma would have a wash at the *thuravu*; just then the whining bell of the Murugan temple would invite her in. Heart melting, Amma would go to the temple. By the time the pooja was over, darkness would have fallen. When she returned home with the *viputhi* and the *santhanam* in the closed palm of her hand, Seelan would have lit all the lamps, making the house glow.

He would be seated at the table, his face blossoming in the lamplight, reading or writing something. The softly playing radio out front would bring him pleasure. The front wheel of the cycle by his side would, slanting gracefully, gaze at him with a bright, effulgent smile.

The daughter was a beautiful bud. Though she was small, she'd be in the kitchen preparing a cup of tea. Only Kulam would not be seen: Amma was unable to state with any degree of certainty when he'd be home. The work he did was of that nature.

The bells round their necks tinkling, the cows would be heard crunching grass, breathing heavily, swishing their tails to drive away flies. The smell of cow dung and the scent of grass would hit the nostrils sharply. The cooped-up fowls would be cackling, noisily beating their wings.

A hot cup of tea after a day's hard work, after worshipping at the temple, just when night was pleasantly beginning to fall . . . Amma would have tea with her marvellous children . . . oh, that was life!

Had everything gone away with Seelan, without even bidding farewell to Amma?

Wearily Amma walked over to the stack of straw.

How, why did children, who had come out of one and the same womb, have such different traits? She had nurtured them both the same way, had fed them both the same way, had sent them both to the same school. She would stand at the threshold savouring the sight of them going to school carrying their school books, their well-oiled hair slicked down.

Kulam was the one who disrupted his studies; he would always fight with his elder brother. Sometimes he would not eat because he was angry with his mother. He could not progress beyond the sixth standard. Amma knew that her younger son was very bright but she could not fathom why he was unable to study.

Seelan studied quietly. He was a very quiet boy. He couldn't raise his voice to talk. Though he treaded softly, his walk had a certain air of dignity about it. His walk would not hurt even the grass. He had large eyes; his palms were soft and cool. His long nails were rose coloured. His fingers too were long, slender and expressive, like a girl's.

Seelan was born on a pleasant evening. After the twitter of the birds had died down, after the cattle had returned home from the grazing grounds, when the kerosene lamps were emitting soft yellow rays of light, Seelan was born, on a day when the moon was waxing, slightly grazing Amma's left thigh. His *natchathiram* was *punarpusam*. "He has been born to perform great deeds," his horoscope predicted.

Kulam's *natchathiram* was *aththa*. Was that why he was endowed with brutish qualities? Astrologers said *aththam* was *adharmam*.

The afternoon was terrible, silent. The Sun's heat drove the wind away. You could roast groundnuts in the layers of the dust in the lanes. The *puvarasu* trees wilted in this cruel heat. People didn't show their heads out of doors. Only mangy dogs, their tongues lolling, ran hither and thither in search of shade. Crows cawing hoarsely flew about in search of water.

Kulam was born on an afternoon. He weighed eight pounds at birth: Amma had writhed in pain during the delivery and lost consciousness. It took a long time for her to regain consciousness. It took several days for the fever to subside.

Somehow Amma had had a much greater liking for Seelan. Even after he had grown taller than her, even after hair had sprouted on his upper lip, Amma took a special delight in stroking the hair on his head which was as downy as a child's.

Kulam's hair was kinky and unruly. His eyes were narrow and

sunken. His body reeked of kerosene, oil and sweat: his job was like that. Kulam had become a mechanic, like his uncle. His job had no fixed or regular hours; sometimes for days at a stretch he wouldn't turn up at home. His meals were irregular. He didn't have time to look after or groom himself. Perhaps because he wanted his elder brother to study, he went on working incessantly without taking a break.

Thinking of this, Amma sighed as if her heart would burst.

Why did Seelan go away like that?

Slowly, Amma pulled out a sheaf of straw from the stack. The dog came running up to her, rubbed its moist nose against her legs and vigorously wagged its tail. Amma raised her leg to kick it away.

Gratitude seemed to ooze out from the dog's eyes. Seelan had brought it. How could she kick it? She lowered her leg.

Seelan had come carrying it during the rainy season on a sluggish day. It had been white in colour. Now it had grown up and turned brown.

It had been thoroughly drenched in the rain and was whimpering and shivering in the wet streets. Its pitiable state, which had not roused sympathy in anyone else, had touched Seelan. He had carried it home and covered it with an *ola* basket. In the manner of one who had accomplished something, he had told his mother. "When it grows up, it'll prove useful ... polecats won't come, Amma ... it'll guard the fowls."

Daily he would milk the red brown cow and feed the dog its milk. He knew which cow's milk was tasty and full of fat.

Amma walked towards the cows. The dog playfully ran behind her, sniffing at her heels, causing her almost to stumble.

The dog was leaping about playfully in its youth. It had grown fat and its body was glistening. Seelan too had grown plump, with full cheeks and magnetic eyes ... how handsome he had become, this Amma's son!

He was quiet; he wouldn't even raise the volume of the radio. The music coming over the radio could be heard only by him; he didn't wish to be a nuisance to others. Even when he was studying, the radio in front of him would be on. Even when he cleaned the bicycle, the radio would keep on singing. Every morning he would polish the bicycle till it shone bright. He would check for air in the tyres and nod his head in satisfaction. There was order in everything he did.

After he was gone, everything bacame disorderly. The radio had fallen silent. The house itself seemed to have become lifeless. The cycle lay untouched and covered with dust; its tyres had become deflated and thin and it had been placed against the wall.

Kulam had no need of the bicycle. He had at his command a variety of vehicles: cars, vans, motorcycles. He would come cleaving the wind in one of these vehicles.

After Seelan left the house, only roughness, silence, and Amma's sighs remained. The daughter was young and innocent; she had not reached the age of understanding, this beautiful little bud.

Why did Seelan leave the house?

Amma had been closely observing Seelan: for some time he had not been his usual self. The examinations too were approaching. He seemed to be thinking seriously about something and to be anxious and concerned about it. Was he worried about the examination? Why, when he had studied hard for them?

He seemed to have become detached from everything. He avoided looking Amma in the eye. He seemed to be muttering something to himself and frequently shook his head. His nights were sleepless: he could be heard tossing about. In the mornings he wouldn't play the radio; all these days Amma had thought he played the radio like a musical instrument, and it was his own sweet, rich voice that came floating in the air . . . that all the pleasurable things in the world had been created for him . . . that all that he touched would glitter . . . that somewhere a rare beauty was growing up for him . . . that they would bring forth beautiful, babbling grandchildren for Amma.

But Seelan seemed to have changed utterly. He went to sit the examinations but he didn't show the enthusiasm or the excitement of the other students. Amma didn't ask him anything, as she didn't want to bother her sweet boy. Whether he had fallen in love or something . . . Let him come out with it in his own time.

The examinations were proceeding and Seelan grow paler by the day. Where had the vivacity on his face vanished? Amma couldn't understand anything.

That particular day Seelan was up early. Somewhere he brushed his teeth carefully for a long time. He went about like a zombie. His firm footprints clearly showed on the compound, which had been swept clean by Amma. She was surprised and asked, "Isn't it getting late, son?" He didn't even eat properly. He got on his bicycle in a calm and controlled manner, unlike his usual way of jumping on to the bicycle and taking off in one go. Seated on the cycle, he checked the tyres for air.

"I'll get going, Amma."

"Pray to God and go."

Even after that, why doesn't he move?

"It's getting late, son."

"I'm going," he murmured bluntly.

He pedalled slowly like an old man. Amma followed him, stepped on to the road and stood watching him go. Before he rounded the bend, he turned his head once and looked back.

Amma went back inside and sat on the *thinnai* for some time. Later, waiting to apply oil and comb her hair, she searched for the bottle of oil. Sensing that someone on a bicycle had come to the entrance, she peeped out. It was Seelan! What on earth had come over him today?

Seelan came inside. Had he forgotten and left something behind?

He sat on the *thinnai*, his face drained of life.

"What is it sonny, is your head aching?"

"No, no." He bent down and began scratching the ground.

"Wait, I'll make you a cup of coffee."

. . .

"Is today's subject difficult?"

He shook his head indifferently.

"Then, why are you like this? What's wrong with you?"

. . .

"Do you need money or something?"

He smiled. What a simpleton this Amma was!

Hurriedly, Amma brought him a cup of coffee. He took it, no, he grabbed it. His eagerness and excitement surprised her. When he took the cup, his fingers touched Amma's hands: there was a firmness in the fingers as never before. His palms were moist with sweat.

"Amma, where is *thangachchi?*"

"She must have gone somewhere hereabouts . . . Why?"

"I just asked."

"Don't wait for her. You should get going. It's getting late."

He stood up immediately as if he had steeled himself for this. For a while he stood still. For a second he gazed at Amma's eyes searchingly.

"I am go . . . ing, Amma."

Abruptly he turned and leapt astride his bicycle and cycled away fast. It was as if some incomprehensible force was separating him from Amma and dragging him away.

Distraught, Amma rushed to the road. Seelan was disappearing round the bend. She expected him to turn and look back once. But he didn't. Only then did Amma notice a small polythene bag hanging from a bicycle handle. The wheels, like a crawling snake, had left behind in their wake a track along the road.

Amma couldn't understand: she raised her eyebrows.

In the evening everything became clear. Hesitantly a boy came wheeling Seelan's bicycle. With bowed head, he leant the bicycle against the wall. Amma remembered having seen him somewhere. He purposely diverted his gaze to avoid looking at Amma's face.

He cleared his throat and said, "Seelan told me to bring this and leave it here."

"*Appu*, where's Seelan?"

. . .

"Aiyo, my child . . ."

The anguish in her voice drove the boy away. His head still lowered, he hastened away.

A stricken Amma shrieked, "*Appu*, where is Seelan?"

Amma ran stumbling after the boy, repeating her question. Unable to reply, the boy began to run.

"Where is Seelan, *Appu?*"

She addressed the question to the chilly wind, which blew past her without answering. It was silent because it had witnessed the grief of so many mothers like Amma.

"Aiyo, where is my Seelan?" she asked the red evening sky streaked by lighting.

It closed its eyes, without speaking: how many such instances had it witnessed!

"Where is Seelan?"

There was no one to give an answer that would satisfy her.

Amma's piteous question beat against the village and stirred it. The womenfolk of the village gathered one by one around Amma.

They knew where Seelan had gone. How many such stories they knew. Supporting Amma, they took her inside.

Along with Seelan, happiness departed from that simple, small home. Only a void remained.

In the evenings Amma would go to the fields, the palmyra groves, and the uplands to cut grass. She would carry the bundles of grass all the way back, panting, her back hurting. There was no one to relieve her of the burden. Halfway on her homeward journey, the whining of the Murugan temple bell would he heard. She was not able to attend the *poojas* at the appointed times. As she passed, the temple would be steeped in silence and darkness. The scattered flowers, the scent of camphor in the breeze, the slow flame of the small lamp and the locked, ornately carved heavy door bore testimony that the *poojas* had been performed.

Amma stood at the entrance and worshipped all alone. Daily she would pray with melting heart for the well being of her beloved son. When she returned home, the cows would be butting and chasing one another in the rear compound. There would be hoofmarks and dung all over the place.

Amma had to drag the cows one by one and tether them.

The fowls had learnt to roost in the *poovarasu* trees. Amma would pick up stones to throw at them; she would try to bring them down from their tree perches by shooing. The cackling of the fowls and the beating of their wings dispelled the silence of the early part of the night.

Amma had to shut them in their cages all by herself.

A small, sooty lamp shed a dim light. On the table lay Seelan's books. A cycle. A radio which had fallen silent. Beside it would be seated a beautiful, small bud. She would sit alone and keep herself awake, her mind filled with precocious thoughts. Poor thing!

Amma did not receive any more that wonderful cup of tea in the evening.

Amma grew thinner. Dark circles appeared round her eyes. Her walk became less steady. Unlike before, she could not eagerly throw herself into her work. Slowly, Amma was growing old.

She spent sleepless nights tossing about trying to get a wink of sleep. Tired of tossing about, she would sit up. She would sigh, as all sorts of untoward thoughts crossed her mind.

Kulam too seemed to become unfathomable to her. He would come home once in three or four days. When partly asleep, she lay tossing about in agony, a vehicle would draw up at the entrance with a roar. Kulam would come in hurriedly. He wouldn't speak a word to her or look her straight in the face. He would thrust some money into her hands. Taking off his shirt, he would carelessly toss it somewhere. He would spread out the ola mat and lie down, without a pillow. Pressing his forehead firmly with his strong hands, wiggling his legs, his chest, on which hair was beginning to sprout, heaving up and down, he would fall asleep in a second.

He's sleeping now, Amma would think, just like that. A jungle creature!

Bomb explosions were frequently heard. Amma trembled when she heard them, her eyes would open wide in fear and the pit of the stomach would begin to rumble.

They would frequently cordon off villages. The moment she heard the roar of heavy vehicles, Amma's life would begin to drain away. When, with guns pointing at her, they asked in threatening tones, "Where is your son," when they rounded up and took away children at gunpoint, Amma's fears could not be expressed in words.

"Oh, God! Please let me see my child once before I die."

Every night bomb explosions would be heard in the village: her eardrums ached as if ready to burst. Her chest felt dry. Oh, these nights were terrible.

The village womenfolk told Amma that the boys were using the fields, the palmyra groves and the uplands—so familiar to Amma—for training in exploding bombs.

Could Seelan be one of them, she thought, greatly alarmed. But not even a dog had told Amma that Seelan had been seen.

In which village was Seelan getting trained in setting off explosions? She did not know much about other villages. Amma's world was the small hut that served as her home, the Murugan temple, the dusty lanes, the palmyra groves, the uplands, the cows and the fowls. Her children were her priceless treasure.

There were frequent bomb explosions this day. With every explosion, the memory of Seelan weighed more heavily on her. Kulam too had not come home for four or five days.

Amma was anxious for him to come home today.

What kind of a son was he? He rarely came home and when he did turn up he went to sleep immediately. "Amma I'm hungry." No, he never uttered these words. How contented a mother feels when she hears a child say it's hungry! This jungle creature couldn't understand even this.

Where does he have his meals?

Amma thought Kulam would definitely come home today. She kept awake on the *thinnakunthu*, her legs outstretched.

The moonlight was dim. The moon looked like a beautiful woman's forehead. Amma was looking at the white clouds speeding across the sky. Even in the dim moonlight, the leaves of the *poovarasu* shone.

Amma was all alone. Soot darkened the lamp's chimney. The daughter was sleeping peacefully. She could hear the cows breathing and the clucking of the fowls. She could see the dog running hither and thither, gasping for breath and scratching the ground.

A cicada began to screech. Without cause, the dog began to bark. It was barking at the moon, she thought.

The red brown cow began to moo unhappily. Something was tormenting it but Amma was unable to get up and go to the rear compound. She sat there, not moving a muscle.

She began to pay attention to the smells, shapes and sounds of midnight. Somewhere a pullanthi must have bloomed. The pungent smell of *kurakkan pittu* picked the nostrils: the smell of a viper when it has caught its prey! The fence rustled: a deadly poisonous viper, its body covered with deceptively beautiful markings was slithering within the fence. Amma was mortally afraid.

When would Kulam come? She frequently prayed to Murugan that Kulam turn up.

The sounds of bombs were frequent. The ground, the air, and the sky vibrated. There was a churning in the pit of her stomach.

How did those, who as children were terrified of the dark and clung to their mothers' sides when they slept, learn to wander about at midnight in the deserted fields where even devils feared to go? How were they able to bear those terrible explosions? How were they able to accept all those dangers with a smile? Who had sowed such intensity and wrath in their minds?

"Oh God! These children whoever gave birth to them ... They go without food ..."

A bomb burst with a discordant sound, a sound unfamiliar and not heard before, a sound odious and disgusting, like the sound of a prematurely born baby before it becomes lifeless.

Amma's body began to sweat. Instinct told her that something bad had happened. She got up and went towards the table. With trembling hands she raised the lamp wick. She stepped down into the compound. Drawing her saree tight around her, she looked in the direction of the explosion. With its tail between its legs, the dog stood beside her. Its ears pricked up and it growled slightly. It began to howl and run round the house fast. It stopped by Amma's feet ... then began to run, as if it were keen to communicate bad news to Amma!

Repeatedly, the red brown cow cried in agony! The pitch of the cicada's dirge increased. The pungent smell of *kurakkan pittu* was all-pervasive.

Worn out, Amma sat down in the compound, her heart quaking. She felt parched. She struggled to breathe as if something heavy were stuck in her throat.

Thoughts of Seelan made her anxious. Her expectation that today at least Kulam would come home had been belied. The night grew blacker and descended heavily all round her and told her something in a mournful voice. In the distance could be heard the sound of a vehicle speeding along the road, as if rushing someone to the hospital.

Somewhere something had gone terribly wrong.

A fowl cried piteously. A polecat must have seized it. Its feeble cry gradually died away in the distance. The dog gave chase but returned unsuccessful.

Her eyes open, Amma had a dream.

Amma stands in a field. The sun beats down mercilessly; it rains too. The rainwater blisters her body. She runs. Panting, she enters the village. The lanes are inundated, like a red-coloured thread a brook of blood mingles with the floodwater. She follows the brook of blood for a long distance. At last she arrives: Seelan is there at the entrance of the house, his head bowed. Blood gushes from his eyes and mingles with the floodwater. There is blood all over the house. The dog is lapping up the blood.

It was inauspicious to dream about blood. Amma wanted to shriek but she couldn't.

Kulam did not turn up at all that day. Amma was wide awake the whole night: every second she experienced the agony of that horrendous night.

The morning star appeared in the eastern sky and drove the moon westwards. The crows announced the dawn with mournful caws. The fowls beat their wings, cackled and crowed, paying tribute to their comrade who had fallen the previous night. The cows, their udders full of milk called to their calves. The sun rose slowly, like a mourner who goes to a funeral house with bowed head.

The daughter who was innocent of the world and its ways came out, shaking off her sleepiness. She gazed uncomprehendingly at her mother who sat still in the compound, holding her chin in one hand. Amma's life seemed to have run away and gone into hiding somewhere. It seemed as if even a gentle breeze would topple her feeble body to the ground.

Slowly Amma got up and sat on the *thinnai*, her legs outstretched. Wouldn't some women with nothing to do come in search of Amma?

Wouldn't Amma then sob out all her grief to her, in a broken voice?

No one came. Instead the daughter had to go to school. The cows had to be untethered and driven to the grazing ground. The fowls had to be attended to. Amma carried out all these tasks like a robot; strain had coarsened her brain. The eyes were burning; a sign that an inner fever was raging in Amma's body. Like a scorching wind, her hot breath singed her lips. Without any reason she would take a few tottering steps and then sit in one place for a long time . . . she would gaze abstractedly into the distance and sigh heavily.

The sun had disappeared without bidding farewell to anyone. The waning moon shone weakly, defeated by darkness. The tired wind walked rather than blew. But Amma couldn't notice any of these.

What has become of Seelan?

Why hasn't Kulam come home for four or five days?

These questions alternated in Amma's mind, one chasing the other. For three days at a stretch bomb explosions were not heard. An ominous silence and quiet enveloped the village. For three days she couldn't eat even a morsel of food. She was hiccuping all the time.

The fourth night fell speedily.

Oh! These cruel nights!

Amma was seated on the *thinnaikunthu*, legs outstretched. The tree leaves, touched by the wind, quivered. The moon occasionally peeped out of the clouds as if afraid of them and then suddenly pulled its head back. Someone smoking a cigar must have gone along the lane: its reek was wafted by the wind. The dog lay curled up by Amma's side.

Amma sensed the coming of a vehicle. Its speed was moderate. It stopped at the entrance, the glare of its lights making the eyes blink. The toot of a horn announced its arrival.

Amma sighed with relief. Thank God! Kulam had come home tonight!

The sound of doors being opened and banged. Not only Kulam, some others too must have come. The sound of whispers! They pushed open the *padalai* gently. They came in as a group.

They brought in someone, half supporting him. Frightened, Amma stood up swiftly. She took the lamp and held it up to see better.

A worn-out Kulam was being brought in. One of those who were supporting him was gently holding Kulam's right hand: below the wrist, a blood-soaked bandage.

Aiyo! What had happened to Amma's roughneck child?

Amma wanted to cry out but couldn't: the tongue had cleaved to the palate. She wanted to move but couldn't, as if someone had nailed her legs to the floor.

They spread out the *ola* mat and placed pillows on it. Groaning in unbearable pain, Kulam lay down. His face was drawn and pallid. His lips were dry and the skin peeling. He was very thirsty. He ran his tongue over his lips. "Amma," he called in a feeble voice but Amma was unable to respond to the call.

The son was suffering from thirst. But Amma was unable to move a step.

They came near and, with bowed heads, they surrounded her. One of them touched Amma. She looked at them with eyes that refused to blink.

Amma identified them: they were the sons who roamed the deserted fields at midnight. Oh, had Kulam too been deceiving his poor, innocent mother all this time?

Shaking her by the shoulders, one of them told Amma, "Make him some coffee."

Her roughneck son, her unfathomable boy, had come back without a hand! He was parched and agonizingly thirsty. Oh God! Won't you give Amma some strength? Amma attempted to ask something, but only a meaningless moan came forth. Amma attempted to move. Striving with all her might she wrenched free her legs. Her whole body ached as if in the agony of death. She took a step forward only to sprain her legs. She fell backwards.

They lifted Amma up, spread out an *ola* mat, and, placing pillows on it, slowly laid her down.

How did the news spread throughout the village?

Hurriedly, kerosene lamps were lit. One by one, the womenfolk of the village gathered in Amma's compound.

"It exploded in the hand," one whispered to another, in a frightened tone. Amma heard this as if in a dream. She turned and looked at

Kulam. Drop by drop crimson blood was staining the pillow. Hot tears ran down Amma's cheeks.

An elderly woman suffering from backache and aging rapidly. Nowadays she does not speak to or smile at anyone in the village.

A beautiful little bud, innocent of the ways of the world; a withering flower plant, her mind filled with precocious fancies, worries and anxieties. More than half of the mother's work has been thrust on her frail shoulders. She does not go regularly to school. Even on the days she attends, she goes late to school: wearing a dirty uniform, her hair tousled, her face wan, her fear of being late reflected in her eyes, clutching her books to her chest, she hurries, half running, half walking through the dusty lanes.

A roughneck young man. One hand has been amputated below the wrist. His comrades frequently visit him. He is an excellent mechanic, a brainy fellow. Indispensable. With one hand he does wonders. Once in four or five days, he comes home at midnight. The severity and the fanaticism evident in his face astound and disconcert one. He is unsociable, a recluse. He doesn't talk much, is tight lipped. As soon as he comes home, he gives money to his mother, spreads out the ola mat and, without even a pillow to lay his head on, goes to sleep.

The small hut, which serves as their home, is very old. The roof has decayed. Piles of *puvarasu* leaves litter the compound.

A dog with no one to care for it; its ribs are showing. It has grown very lean and ... armies of ticks have invaded its ears and made them droop downwards. It has dug a hole somewhere in a corner of the compound and lies curled up there. It neither barks nor runs. It'll die soon.

Cattle brokers frequently come to the house and drag a cow or a calf away: spreading its legs out it bellows, refusing to go. It calls to Amma for help; it appeals to its kin. All the cows bellow piteously.

In the nights, bombs are frequently heard. Polecats seize the fowls by their throats and carry them away, crying out in pain. The fowls' cries grow weaker and weaker and fade away in the distance.

Bomb explosions don't bother Amma now. She has become accustomed to sorrows and losses. Carrying the horoscopes of Kulam and

Seelan she goes in search of reputed astrologers.

Seelan was born under the *punarpoosa natchathiram*. Rama too was born under that zodiacal sign; Rama too was destined to live in forests, to cross the sea, to fight incessantly against *adharmic* enemies. He defeated those arrogant beings in the South of Ceylon, who thought they were invincible. He granted salvation to those who suffered from a curse. He too transcended differences: the monkey and the huntsman were his comrades. But oh, those who loved Rama had to suffer the pangs of separation from him: Dasaratha, Kosalai, Sita.

Kulam was born under the *aththa natchatiram*. The astrologers said the sign was *adharmic*. They said he would indulge in treasonable activities and have to face severe *kandams*. They said his horoscope showed he might even end up in jail, and that all the planets were debilitated.

Translated by A J Canagaratna

The Gap

THAMARAICHCHELVI

His mind had been restless over the past few days. Did he have to endure this life of mental agony at the age of seventy-two? He woke up in the dark of the early morning and sat wondering whether it had ever crossed his mind that he might undergo such pain of mind in his old age. Now every morning brought him frustration and dejection.

Thoughts of his days in Kumaarapuram before this displacement surged in his mind. His heart longed for the sound of the bell that tolled at five in the morning at the Murugan Temple. How sweet were those morning hours! All that had become a thing of the past since he moved to Skandapuram. What remained were pressures of survival and fears for the future.

He stared into the dark for a while. The sleeping bodies lay in a row along the veranda looking like lines in the dark. He sat with his legs stretched out on the ground and rubbed his face with his thin hands.

The air was still a little warm. It was stuffy inside his mind as well. The pouch that his fumbling fingers picked up from under his mattress was empty. The tobacco ran out yesterday, and he couldn't ask his son for money. He would only grumble, "You are munching tobacco as if it were food," and that would hurt his feelings.

Only after his beard grew into white bristles making his face unpresentable would his son offer him some money, saying, "Father, take this and go and get a shave." To stretch out his hand to his son for every single thing seemed a very harsh situation to be in.

Conditions had not been this way when he lived in the village. The income had been good from the coconut, banana and mango trees that filled his garden. There was, besides, the lease money from the paddy land to the west of the village. There was ample to eat and what a right royal life it was—a life with honour and respect in the village.

It was a great joy to sip the hot tea his wife Paakiyam served him when he returned from the temple after the evening puja and a leisurely chat in the temple hall with people of his vintage.

It was also a great comfort to live in the house that he had built of stone and earth through his own efforts. Although he had to cook his own meals after Paakiyam passed away, he had never suffered as much pain as he did now.

His only son Paramu was running a small business in Kilinochchi and decided to live there with his wife and three children. There was no need for Paramu to look after him as he had enough money to attend to his needs. Even at the time he was forced to leave Kumaarapuram, on the twenty-sixth of July the previous year, he had three thousand rupees in his pocket.

The way the shells were fired that day made it impossible for him to get to Kilinochchi. So he collected what he could and fled to Kunjup Paranthan village. It was only after he had reached Skandapuram on foot that Paramu asked him to stay with his family.

That piece of land was obtained with the help of someone known to Paramu. When, initially, a little shed was erected there, he gave the Paramu money he had on him. A bedroom, a kitchen adjoining it, and a veranda at the front with a plastic canopy over it—that was the house and the little space on the left of the veranda was his patch. There were, apart from him, his son's mother-in-law, her three sons, and the family of her eldest daughter. All of them in this little house.

It had been a year since he came here but his mind was not willing to accept this stressful existence. The life of displacement was burdened with too many difficulties. There was no more the comfort of stretching out at the entrance hall of his own house. He could hardly move on either side of his little space on the veranda, with his daughter-in-law's brothers and her sister's husband lying there in a row along the veranda. If it rained, the spray from the rain drenched him where he lay.

The well at the rear of the property provided water for bathing and cooking. The people in the neighborhood also used it. To get drinking water, one had to walk a mile. It was he who filled two plastic cans with water, hung them on either side of the bicycle with a piece of rope, and pushed the laden bicycle home.

Usually it took a while for the meals to be ready. Eating rice in the evenings caused him heartburn. But it had been rice and curry mix even for dinner, and that too served only after the children had eaten. His hunger would have surged and subsided by the time he ate. He hadn't the heart to fault his daughter-in-law: after all, there were so many in the house.

He had had two attacks of malaria since he arrived in Skandapuram, and the bitter taste that malaria caused in his mouth lingered. Now it was not only his body but also his mind that was beginning to weaken and, especially over the past few days, he had often wondered whether he had become an unbearable burden to the household.

Paramu had a little shop at the intersection in Skandapuram, and when he was home he would give vent to his frustrations at the lack of business in the shop. While he understood that Paramu's anger and fury were born of desperation, he was in no position to help. Having to depend on Paramu for everything, he suffered in silence.

With such a son, what could he expect of the daughter-in-law! From dawn to dusk, he did whatever he could for the family. The fear that they might feel that he was a burden on them was always there at the back of his mind. He would do everything, from going to the shops and the market, to taking the parboiled paddy for milling, to collecting drinking water. But there was never a word of appreciation from his daughter-in-law.

Although there were so many in the house, he always felt alone. At midday, all would gather in the shade of the margosa tree in the lawn at the front, but he could not. Even when he chose to attend to something on his own, there was likely to be some hindrance.

Fridays troubled him. At Kumaarapuram he used to go to the Murugan Temple without fail for the midday service. Since arriving here, he started to visit the Skandapuram Murugan Temple, a ten-minute walk from the house. But it was a big struggle to have a bath at the well.

Women from the neighbourhood gathered by the well in the morning to bathe before they prepared the meal to end their Friday morning fast. Towel in hand, he would hang around until eleven. His daughter-in-law would tell his grandson, "Ramanan, tell granddad to have his bath after the women have had theirs." Her words would stir anger in his heart. "These women who come to bathe just hang around all day with a cloth round their bodies. Can I wait that long?" He would fume, swallow his words.

Unable to suffer any longer, Friday last week he rushed to the well and started to bathe. It seemed as if he had committed sacrilege. "Dad, did you have to go when the women were there? Could you not have had your bath a little later?" Paramu yelled at him. "Why?" He wanted to respond. "Don't they all bathe together in the canal? Besides, can't they start their cooking a few minutes later? I don't want to be late for the midday pooja." But he didn't say a word.

As it was he who usually went to the shops and to the market, he was the one who brought the coconuts. His daughter-in-law would demand in an agitated voice, "Did you have to pay twenty rupees for this unripe nut?" It would be useless to explain that only unripe nuts were on sale.

He would walk back home with his purchases in the scorching sun at eleven, and as he walked in his daughter-in-law would demand, "There is no tamarind in the house. Can you buy some?" He would suppress his anger and tell her calmly "Child, can't you give me a complete list when I set out?" Her face would change colour, a sure sign that trouble was in store when Paramu returned that evening. The expression on her face would not change until Paramu chided his father "What else do you have to do here? Is it so difficult to walk to the market just there? Why do you have to talk back instead of doing what you are told?"

Invariably, he would have to walk to the market twice or thrice a day, thanks to her forgetfulness. But he couldn't show his anger.

Paramu's eldest son Paarthiban was eighteen and in the GCE Advanced Level at a school in Akkaraayn. He had too many friends. Around sunset they would gather beneath the mango tree by the fence. What they spoke made no sense to him and names like Rambaa, Meenaa and Rojaa were totally unfamiliar.

He thought that he had recognized one of the lads. So he dared to ask him, "Son, where are you from?" to which the boy replied, rather hesitantly, "Vattakkachchi then and Maniyankulam now." "Where in Vattakkachchi? What is your father's name? What is he doing now?" he probed further. The boy's face darkened and he turned aside. Paarthiban stared hard at the grandfather.

No sooner had his friends left, than Paarthiban pounced on him, "Granddad, why do you keep asking these questions? Can't you keep your mouth shut!"?

"What have I said wrong, child? Is it wrong to ask one about his father?" He protested meekly. He could not make much sense of all this.

"Isn't there a time and a place for such questions? His father has abandoned the family and is carrying on with a woman from Mallaavi. How do you expect him to feel when you keep probing him? He was sure to think that you knew everything and asked him on purpose."

That shocked him and his voice choked as he replied, " How was I to know? I asked out of politeness."

Paramu for his part added, "Why should you conduct inquiries with his friends? Do you need to know all the gossip in town? Rather than keeping your mouth shut in your old age."

Something seemed to shatter within him. His heart was still agitated, as he replied, "So, if one is old he has to keep his mouth shut."

Another day, he had spotted Paarthiban with his friends at the entrance to a mini-cinema and faithfully reported it at home. When Paarthiban came home at half past nine in the evening, Paramu swore at him, "I pay the fees for your private tuition, and you go to see Arunaachalam. Does money grow on trees?" He followed this with a sound thrashing. That day onwards Paarthiban saw in his grandfather an enemy and would mutter, "The old codger has sneaked . . ." for him to hear.

Paramu's second child, Nandhini, would go with her friends to bathe in the canal rather than at the well. He did not approve of this, and Nandhini did not like his telling her "Why do you have to bathe in the canal? You can bathe here at the well". She would look at him sternly and slap his tumbler on the table with a thud whenever she served his tea.

Ramanan, the youngest, was eight. Although he too quarrelled with the grandfather, he would make up in no time. Whenever the grandfather went for his bath, his mother would urge Ramanan, "Go, go. Have your bath along with granddad!" Often it was he who bathed Ramanan and spent time with him. But since yesterday Ramanan too had been cross with him.

It was before break of dawn yesterday and still dark. He had got up and seated himself on a tree stump beneath the margosa tree and lit his cigar. He heard Ramanan moan, "Mummy, I want to go to the toilet." His mother responded, "Go ahead." "I am scared." "Alright, I will come along".

Ramanan, still half asleep, opened the front door and stepped out, only to find a dark figure with a little red glow. He screamed aloud "O mother! Ghost!" and ran back. For the next five minutes or so, the whole house was in a state of turmoil.

"Why did you have to sit in the dark and frighten the child?" His daughter-in-law's accusation struck him with a sting.

"The kid has got really scared. He may even catch fever." Paramu's anxiety hurt him. But he still could not see what was wrong about smoking a cigar on his own. Since that incident, he felt that Ramanan was keeping a distance from him because he thought that his grandfather sat under the tree on purpose.

Why couldn't they accept him for what he was? As he wondered about these contradictions, a strange sense of fear stirred in his mind. "I am a destitute with no one to turn to," he thought. His eyes welled with tears. The very thought of the plight of having to sit up and ponder his unfortunate situation in the morning was unbearable to his heart.

He stared into the dark that lay ahead. The house was quiet. There were one or two people on the road and he could hear the roar of a distant motorbike. His mouth itched for tobacco. He got up and spat out the saliva from his bitter-tasting mouth and sat down again. His helplessness and desperation joined forces to arouse within him a sense of fury. His mind searched for ways of expressing that feeling.

"I do so much for this house, from buying bread in the morning to mending the gate. From now on, I shall do nothing." This decision crystallized in his wandering mind to give it some consolation.

"Is it not the duty of the son whom he fathered, raised and protected in every way for so many years to look after him and feed him in his old age?" His mind demanded with pride. "Did I demand work from my son to bring him up?"

It was dawning slowly and he started to attend to his matters. He washed his face, walked up to the rack on the veranda, collected a bit of holy ash from the rack and applied it on his forehead. The thought came to his mind that he could go for a walk to the Pillayaar Temple in Karumbuthottam. He picked up his two-yard dhoti from the coir rope line stretched across the vegetable patch, wrapped it around his waist, slung a towel across his shoulder and set out.

No sooner had he got near the margosa tree on the lawn, than Ramanan came running after him calling "Granddad! Granddad!"

"What . . . ?" He stopped and turned back. "Granddad, Amma wants you to buy two loaves of bread. Here is the money and take this bag."

"I can't. Go away. Is it not enough that I bought bread all these days? Why can't one of you do it? Only then will you all appreciate my worth . . ." He thought of saying this, but his voice let him down.

He hesitated a moment, took the money and the bag and walked towards the shop at the intersection.

Translated by S Sivasegaram

To Grandmother

V I S JAYAPALAN

Hands of palm trees
framing the waves
perennial as you
my grandmother

Demons possessing
you relentlessly
have all now fled

On the ashes of the Portuguese
rise the coconut trees
fruits for us to pick
from the coconut trees

On the graves of those
victors by chance
defying time,
my grandmother lives

Again on your shores
have they appeared
the vanquished Portuguese?
Speak not of their skin
the colour of their eyes
they are the Portuguese

They shall not remain
a consoling thought

we will prevail.
The Portuguese will die
the palm trees will grow
a consoling thought

Grandmother
in my youth
I danced and sang and romped
and pined
a life that tortoiselike
along your shores I hid
the moon that joined in stealth
to pick those fruits
the sun that joined to splash
in rain-fed pools
all these I leave
for those I love

Rudderless, anchorless
a sailor adrift
on rafts
I dream of your shores

A consoling thought
is all that I possess
you will triumph.

Translated by Chelva Kanaganayakam

Amma, Do Not Weep

CHERAN

Amma, do not weep.
There are no mountains
to shoulder your sorrow
no rivers
to dissolve your tears.

The instant he handed you
the baby from his shoulder,
the gun fired.

On your *tali*, lying there in the dust,
blood spread.

In the heat of the splintering bomb
all your bright dreams withered.

What splattered from your anklet
were neither pearls
nor rubies:
there is no longer a Pandyan king
to recognize blood guilt.

On sleepless nights
when your little boy stirs restlessly
screaming out, "Appa".
what will you say?

When you pace the night, showing him the moon

and soothing him against your breast,
do not say,
"Appa is with God."

Tell him this sorrow continues
tell him the story of the spreading blood
tell him to wage battle
to end all terrors.

Translated by Lakshmi Holmström

Yaman

CHERAN

The wind falters
as fear
fills the night.
I gasp
at the stillness
between the stars.

Whose shadow lurks by the door?

I wouldn't know,
nor would they.
It happened
swiftly.

Death

No reason
no justice
values and virtues
freeze where they stand
in the oppressive silence.

In the dark
lost in flight
pigeons
pound and pound again
against the door.
My resolve to endure
slips.

Yaman

Do the butterflies
disdaining life
shed their colours
in the prime of youth?

As sunflowers
their golden petals
untouched by dust,
lotus flowers
that bloom at the
touch of water;
as stars,
they will be
born again.

Until then
at the edge of the lake,
stare at the waves.

Note: Yaman, in Hindu myth, is the god of death.

Translated by Chelva Kanaganayakam

A New Tamil Bread

SOLAIKKILI

On that day
when wheels sprouted
all over us,
fervour of bees sucking nectar
with the speed of those defying life
we crawled
we crawled
One . . . two . . . three
In less time than it takes to eat a sweet
we travelled far
for humans
it would take two days.

Do you understand?
Put this way you will not,
come on!

You
have tasted stale poems
New poetic bread
in Tamil
you will not understand
will not find sweet.

Listen
I speak of our long journey on
bicycles
Two others with me

a cycle for each
yes
one for me, too
we crawled and crawled as joy
spread like forests
on our heads.

To gather stones from the moon
to build your house
go with feverish haste on your bicycles
in the time it takes to eat a sweet
it will happen
Your teeth too will break
as the heavenly breeze blows.

Translated by Chelva Kanaganayakam

Famine

S SIVASEGARAM

Our parched earth
eats the sun
inhales hot air
excretes dust
in the abandoned fields.

The shrubs the sun spared
the cattle ate.
The cattle that survived
we ate.
Our wide-open eyes
once looked out for the moon
and the street for our guests.
Now they stay awake
dreading trucks and planes.
We once fought in the name of honour
but now for fallen bread crumbs.

Mr NGO takes pictures
of dried-up breasts
that cheat the child
struggling to keep apart the hollow cheeks,
its bloated stomach,
its heaving ribs,
and its eyes that search deep within the skull.
Paste them on the begging bowls.
Let the coins that fall
still the conscience

of those that throw them.
Let them be the evidence
of the greatness of your civilization
Let them be the cross
planted atop the grave of our pride.

We appeal
to the leaders and the owners of the land
that dumps grain in the sea
and to the gentlemen
who bury fruit deep underground
and watch over mountains of meat and butter:
We want not
your generosity nor your grain,
your eggs, butter
blankets and clothes.
Simply stop
dropping arms and ammunition
in the begging bowls
of those who ride on our hunched backs.
That alone will do.
Even if we die today, starved of your shower
of kindness,
tomorrow we shall rise from the dead.

Translated by the author

Do You Understand What I Write?

OORVASHI

It is of no use
to send this letter
to any address that I know.
Nevertheless, somehow or the other
it must reach you.
That you will certainly receive it
is my unshakeable belief.

Here, in the front courtyard
the jasmine is in full bloom.
Honey birds by day
and the scent-laden breeze by night
reach as far as our room.
All sorts of people whom I do not know
walk past out house, often.
Yet, till now, no one has come
to interrogate me.

The small puppy runs in circles
around the house
without reason,
its tail raised high
as if it wants to catch someone.

At night, when I cannot sleep,
I dust your books and put them away.
I have read most of them now.
I have never opened
your mother's letters.

the weight of her grief for her sons
I cannot endure.

And then, my love,
the thought that you have gone away
only for our people's sake
is my only consolation.

Although this imprisoning sorrow is huge,
yet, since our separation,
I have learnt to bear everything.

One thing more:
it is this, most of all
I wanted to say.

I am not particularly a soft-natured woman
nor am I as naive as I once was.
Our current state of affairs
gives me no signs for hope.
It is certain
that for a long time
we must be apart.
Then
why should I stay within this house
any longer?
Well,
Do you understand what I write to you?

Translated by Lakshmi Holmström

The Grief-stricken Wind

S VILVARATNAM

The village lies frozen stiff.
It's been like this
Ever since the morning
The ghostly emptiness
Numbed the sun.

The wind that had slumbered
In the village backyard
Gradually stirred awake.
Cracking its knuckle joints
Stretching its limbs
It emerges slowly.

The empty dust tracks,
The tread of heavy boots
Blurring the footprints
Puzzled the wind.

The rhythm of *ekel*-brooms
Sweeping the compounds,
The sound of bangles
Scraping against scrubbed utensils,
The affectionate calls
For *aachi, appu,* and *amma*
All had vanished.

What had happened?
Why had the village lost its voice?

The stupefied wind
Stood stock-still
Like a small boy
Who had dozed off
Near the *ther*
Awakens dazed
By the silence
After the *thiruvila.*

The wind
Which used to freely enter
Any open entrance
As if it owned the house
Now stood hesitant.
With trepidation
It peeped
Into a house
Not even the hum
Of a human.

It peeped
Into another entrance
No trace of a human
Yet another entrance
No trace of a human.
As it peeped
Into another entrance
The wind heard
Laboured breathing.
It went close.

As the entrance
Lay fallen
An old human
Who had slipped.
Its walking stick

Out of reach
Words struggled
To come out of its mouth
Its breathing failed.
The trembling wind
Looked past the gate
Hoping help would come
Not a soul in sight.

What could the wind do?
If a wail arose
It could carry the lament
Through the length and breadth
Of the village
But there wasn't even a sob
Tears welled up in the wind.

The spirit had left the body
But no kith or kin
To feed it milk
Hold its legs and hands
Sing a *thevaram*.

The spirit had departed unceremoniously
Leaving the body desolate, forlorn
Without a lit oil lamp
Without tomtom beats
Without a *paadai*.

Even in death
The village had life-enhancing ritual.
"Where have all its kith and kin gone?"
The wind asked helplessly
It hovered uncomprehendingly.

How could the wind know

The people
Had sneaked out of the village
Their belongings bundled up in gunnies

In the dead of night
When it was slumbering?
Sighing deeply
The wind went back inside
And hunching like a crone
Sat beside the corpse.
Then it came out
Burying its face
In the folds of its saree.
Pushing towards the fence
A thorny bush peeping into the street
The wind walked slowly
Like a grief-stricken mother
Searching for her runaway son.

Translated by A J Canagaratna

Lament for a Rudely Plucked Sunflower

S VILVARATNAM

Look at this stalk
That grieves inconsolably
Over the heart
Torn from it.
Have you looked?
If you have eyes, look.

Who wrenched it away?
Only a devil's hand
Will stretch out
To rudely pluck
A heart–flower
That quickens
With the sun, its beau ideal

Behold that plucked heart
Beating within myself
That's split and sundered
Like torn-up water lilies.

You do not know
The tremulousness
Of the stalk
Steeped in its memories
Of the flower
That's been plucked.

Till I gather up
The scattered fragments

Of my self
And let it twine, creeperlike
Around my kith and kin
My hands too
Will be pricked
By thorns.

Keep your distance!
Take your hand away,
You devil!
Long-nailed to pluck and tear!
Why did you trespass
Into the zone

Where our life linked lies?
Why did you sunder
Our umbilical cord's lotus
Through which streams
The blood of our forebears?

You miserable wretch
Who trampled on
The strangled children
Whose mouths had blossomed
Into sweet smiles!
You who are congenitally deaf
To the soft cries
Of suckling babes
Away!

Keep away, you iron-fisted one
Who have torn out
The heart of my village
Fresh as the dawn.

Get away, far away

From the boundaries
Of our life zone.

Not for devils
Are our flower parks
Not for uprooting
Are our life-blossoms.

Let each eye bud open
In its own course
Do not pluck
The petals full of honey

Away, you devils!
That the deep-rooted trees
In our groves
May break into flower.

Translated by A J Canagaratna

Express This Grief in Song?

RASHMY

Express this grief in song?

Distance the poem from the tears?

To war
we've offered
our necks and our lives;
our poems then must
reek of the slaughter house?
Have you ever listened
to the howls
and death screams
of those
whose genitals
have been crushed
by jackboots?
Have you listened
to the dying moans
of those
whose vaginas have been ripped apart?
Can your feeble words
console the wails
for those tossed into
abandoned wells
of lavatory pits
or unmarked graves?
Who are the sorcerers
whose talismans

can save us from being haunted
by the wailing spirits
of our sons and daughters
who fight and perish
in the abattoirs?
The innocents
blown to bits
on the streets
along with their dreams?

Can you shoo away
the dog with a dribbling tongue
or drive away
the buzzing flies
from your poetry?

Tell me
how did we learn
to sprout again
from the cinders?
How did we learn
to forget annihilation?
How did we learn
to dust off the ashes,
enjoy carnal pleasures
and skywards soar?
Tell me
What does this mean?

Translated by S. Pathmanathan

Life Lost

R MURALEESWARAN

Renouncing everything
sagelike
the people evacuated,
they craved only for a boon,
the boon of living once again.

In a soil where huts have sprouted
a widowed mother sits
inhaling darkness.
Her hands supports her head
her eyes stare skywards.
Reports said
her son lay buried
at Chemmani.
Reports said
her relatives
 lost their money
to the boatman at Rameshwaram
and their lives
to Yama, the God of Death.
Why then
Does she look heavenwards?

She could look
at the earth
which coffined her son
or at the sea
which devoured

her dear ones.
Why then does she look heavenwards?
Perhaps she is searching for
the life she's lost.

Translated by S Pathmanathan

They Will Come Again!

CASTRO

I am fed up
this is the third time
they have come
it is the third time
they have searched
my baggage
torn my bags
scattered my clothes
glared at me
suspiciously.

it's the third time
they've rubbed, scratched, scrutinized
the same Identity Card
they issued me.

Later
they subjected me
to a body check
at gun point.
My shrunken self-respect
fell dead
like a scorched worm.

One of them
must have thought
of Jesus' counsel.
He slapped me on the left cheek

and before I could turn my right cheek
slapped it too.

When they left
they spirited away
some of my possessions.
They returned
a fourth time.
they'll come again!

Translated by S Pathmanathan

Meeting and Parting

CHERAN

These separate us:

Long mountain ranges,
a rainbow,
an invisible sun
endlessly falling
winter rain,
the proud light
of my dark face.

These unite us:

The heartbeat of waves,
an endless telephone wire
which falls across continents and oceans,
and,
too frightened to question the future,
a tender heart.

Translated by Lakshmi Holmström

When Our Peace Is Shattered

BALASOORIAN

Dust rises in the streets.
Sounds of gun shots cease,
Guns disappear in waist belts,
Jeeps growl,
Dust rises.

Wind swallows
Grief.
The streets
Fill with blood,
Flies fall
And wither on the earth.
Sometimes
A street dog
Lifts its tail and sniffs.

All the same
The world stands still
Embracing the peace.

In an instant
Gun shots will explode
The quiet will shatter
Flies
And street dogs, sometimes,
Will take up arms.

The wind, grief-laden

BALASOORIAN

Will shudder,
As if to say
"That is the way it is
in between times."

Translated by Lakshmi Holmström

The Worship Scar

S VILVARATNAM

After my friend
Introduced his father
Casually
I asked about the scar.
"It's the worship scar",
The *periyavar* said
Stroking his forehead,
His eyes lighting up.
I bit my tongue
Grieved

By my ignorance.
Calling for Allah
He had bowed
Till his native soil
Scarred
His humbled forehead.
Whence sprang my impudence
That dared chase them away
From the soil of their birth
Striking
Their worship scarred forehead
With a hammer?
How thus could I
Injure myself?

Their worship scar
Seared

My guilt-stricken conscience scar.
Like the third eye
They grilled and drilled
My battle field scars too.
When, oh when will my scar
Disappear?
When, oh when will my crime
Of violating the soil's beauty
Etched on their foreheads
Be expiated?
When from exile
They return home
And full-throatedly
Calling for Allah
They renew their worship scars
And stroke their foreheads
The tears dammed up
For years and years
Will burst the eye-dykes.
Only at the moment
I immerse myself
In that cleansing cataract
Will my blemish
Recorded by history
Be washed clean.
That moment only
Will consummate
My liberation.
Friend,
Allah have I entreated
To hasten
That sweet moment
Of reconcilement.

Translated by A J Canagaratna

A War-torn Night

SIVARAMANI

Our children
grow
in the oppression
of a war-torn night.

Faceless and bloodied
corpses
thrown across their
sun-lit dawns;
walls crumbling
around their joy
kids cease to be
children.

The silence of a
starry sky
shattered
the sound of guns
the memory of childhood
disappears.

Making toys
playing games
forgotten
in benighted days.

They learn
to shut the gates

listen
to the strange
barks of dogs.

To not ask
to be silent
when questions remain
unanswered,
they learn
to be mute,
to pluck the wings
of dragonflies
to fashion guns
from sticks
and kill friends turned foes;
these games
they learn.

In the oppression
of a war-torn night
our children grow.

Translated by Chelva Kanaganayakam

Humiliation

SIVARAMANI

Behind the bars
of your laws
I cannot be held;
from your muddy
permanence
I am a stone
reclaimed,
you cannot steal
my day.

Between those fingers
that cover your eyes,
a tiny star
my presence emerges
steadies itself.

I cannot be spurned.
A question
not to be ignored,
I have emerged.
Shroud me with
insults and
abuse.

Upon
your elegant dream,
a mound of dirt;
on your shining shoes

Humiliation

a heap of dust.

Until my claims
are met
all your paths will be
forever dirty.

Translated by Chelva Kanaganayakam

Summer

SELVI

Evening sky;
the light fades
the waves
caress the shore,
the burnt tips
of grass
that skirt the lake
tickle the feet.
The fields to the west
empty and silent
gaze at the sky;
a warm air
ruffles the skin.

The white sand
sparkling in the yard
hurts the eyes.
In the fruit-laden
mango tree
The koel sings
intermittently.

Cobbles on the street
pierce the skin
learn the taste of blood
stones on the edge
chuckle with scorn.

Summer

Thoughts soar and
the heart aches.
The chill of the wind
the green of the spreading
jackfruit tree
fish startled
jump across
the dams.
Sweet thoughts
now eclipsed
oppress the heart
silently.

Translated by Chelva Kanaganayakam

Faces

UMA VARATHARAJAN

Eight days more for the end of month.

He took a piece of paper and noted down the places he would visit. He also drew a map to suit the bicycle ride. The fourteen houses he would visit were scattered. He would have to pedal sixteen miles today.

He could sit in the shop smoking Gold Leaf cigarettes as usual. The tea kiosk opposite would play Susheela's film hits and he could listen. By 1.30 pm the Mahavidyalayam would close and it would take fifteen minutes for the students to disperse. But this month too he had to be prepared to forego two thousand rupees. The company for which he worked would show no mercy either to him or to those fourteen houses. It was his duty to collect the monthly instalments from its customers in the area. He should be ready to pay the total sum by the end of the month.

Nagulan pulled out fourteen cards four by eight inches in size and arranged them. They carried the customers' names, addresses, their purchases, their numbers, the amount paid, balance due, and other important information. Nagulan also used the cards as table mats whenever he ordered in tea from the kiosk. He first closed the windows and then the doors. The company would not approve of this. Perhaps in two days' time the District Manager might send a note along the following lines:

> Under no circumstances should your point be closed. I am very perturbed over your attitude and the excuse given cannot be accepted. If your assistant has gone on leave, you should have made other arrangements.

Once before he had got a note from the DM. His assistant, Manoharan, had also seen it but there has been no change in his routine of going home on Fridays and returning either on Tuesday or Wednesday.

By this time Manoharan might be at the Sinhalawadi Junction seriously involved in an argument over whether it was Rajani's men or Amitabh Bachchan's men who tried to throw acid at Kamalahasan.

The scorching sun was frightening. It would become worse in a couple of hours.

The Raleigh bike started to move. Beyond the bend lay the straight road which Nagulan loved. His apartment, the Irrigation Office, the Police Station, Rohini's house were all on that road.

The road was beautiful in the mornings. A love scene enacted in this setting with Mohan and Suhasini playing the leading roles would be great! Except in the mornings and evenings the vehicles, the heat, the dust and the darkness dominated the road.

Rohini's house always gave the impression of being submerged in a tragic silence. A paddy field lay between it and the road. Nagulan would never be able to see Rohini again. Her Headmaster had spoken to him the other day.

This is an injustice committed from the time of our epics!

Just before the school closed for the summer vacation, she had said goodbye to him and her studies.

Next came Nagulan's house. He had no need to go into his house. Sasi might have been having her breakfast. She might offer him the glass of milk which he had forgotten to take in the morning. It might cause a stomach upset.

Instead of drinking milk for health it appeared to him that he had been doing it out of compulsion. Not only milk, every act in his life seemed to be done under compulsion.

He leaned his bike on an *alari* tree near the Police Station and walked towards the quarters.

Mrs Jayasekera was at home as usual. A message had to be sent to her sergeant husband who was a sergeant.

Mrs Jayasekera was all smiles when she beckoned him to sit. Having settled down, he took out the relevant card. The balance due was two hundred and seventy-five rupees.

Mrs Jayasekera's Sinhala speech was punctuated by her laughter.

Nagulan understood her complaint; she was not satisfied with the board. Could he exchange it for a bright Thailand product? Conversing with Mr Jayasekera was no problem. Except for his typical pronunciation, his Tamil was tolerable. Nagulan had no alternative but to patiently listen to everything. Mrs Jayasekera was obviously irritated. She got up and walked towards the kitchen.

Sergeant Jayasekera walked in briskly, greeting him. He sat opposite Nagulan, "Good Morning," said Nagulan. Not being sure whether the sergeant had heard him, he repeated, "Good Morning!" Sasi used to find fault with him often for mumbling.

Cannot speak to Jayasekera in a curt manner. The type of work he was engaged in needed the help of people like Jayasekera. When a customer, having bought a bicycle, absconded for five months, it was Jayasekera who helped Nagulan trace him.

Jayasekera briefed Nagulan of the day's news in the *Dinamina*. The expulsion of Dr Neville Fernando was right he said. He wanted to know Nagulan's views. Nagulan needed two thousand rupees by the end of the month. "Right," said Nagulan. The sergeant wanted to know his views about the Tiger Movement. Nagulan could only smile. Though Jayasekera was in the Police force, it could not be denied that he had some special qualities.

Whenever Jayasekera dropped in at Nagulan's shop to meet him or pay him, Nagulan would offer to buy him tea. He would decline. Perhaps he thought that would be tantamount to accepting a bribe. But there was one thing he had been asking him: "Change the beard." "That can be done," Nagulan had said. He didn't understand how it could be done.

Jayasekera asked him about his beard. To Nagulan the switch from the Tiger Movement to his beard sounded odd. If he said "I'm sporting a beard because Rohini likes it," the sergeant's enthusiasm would be dampened.

Sipping the coffee Mrs Jayasekera had brought, he told Jayasekera, "The balance outstanding is two hundred and seventy- five rupees."

"Yes, yes," said Jayasekera without interest. "I'll pay on the twenty-fifth. Any problem?"

Nagulan was obliged to say "No." With a "thank you" he took his leave.

As he walked up to his bicycle Nagulan saw a man hurrying to the Police Station. His forehead was bleeding and there were blood stains on his shirt. If he waited any longer he might have to witness somebody carrying his own head!

Now to Onthachimadam. His customer Jeyaraman wouldn't be there. Each time, when he became tired of ringing the bell, the customer's wife would peep through the door. Then she would withdraw. A few agonizing moments. Then she would send word through the neighbour: "No men at home!"

He had pedaled pretty fast and was at Onthachimadam in good time. He was himself in doubt when he rang his bicycle bell.

Inside, in the two-in-one, Shivaji and Manjula were making love: "I didn't know what to do in the precarious situation. That's why I behaved like that. Forgive me, Radha!"

Nagulan, who was in the sun, could guess what would have happened and what Manjula's reply would be. As Nagulan banged the gate someone inside would have strangled Shivaji and Manjula. The gate was opened by Jayaraman himself. Perhaps he might now regret having opened the gate.

"Hello Manager, what brought you here?"

The payment was due on the fifteenth. A week late, and he has the audacity to ask me why I came!

"Nothing in particular . . . just for a chew of betel," said Nagulan sarcastically.

"Come in, why stand in the hot sun?"

Nagulan leaned his bicycle against the fence and went in.

"Jeyaraman! The company van is close by. Keep the machine ready to avoid going to the Police!" said Nagulan. Jeyaraman wasn't shaken by this bombshell. He knew well how many times the van had actually followed Nagulan.

"Manager! Please hold on for some more time. I shall settle my dues in full next month. You see, I was in a mess last month."

Nagulan was furious. "Who decides the installments—you or I? When they come to confiscate the goods, you people become very meek. But now I have to go after you. What do you think I am—your slave?

Jeyaraman was getting nervous. "Quiet brother, I wouldn't have failed to pay if money was available!"

"All this is unnecessary talk," Nagulan interrupted. His tone changed. "Look here. You don't understand our problems. Whether you pay or not, we have to pay at the end of the month. If ten customers default like you, how much have I got to pay out of my own pocket? I don't have a tree in the backyard that bears money!"

"Give me two days. I myself will call over to pay."

He was silent for sometime.

"Upon your word?"

To wriggle out of the present situation, he would even swear by camphor. Nagulan got up.

"This is my last warning. I won't return after this. If the Company confiscates the goods, you will forgo even the installments paid. Understood?"

The bike started moving. If he took the gravel road he would reach a school. It would be interesting to know if the school building was completed or if the thatched roof was still there.

He had been to that school as a Work Supervisor three years ago. That was when he was working in a construction firm. Nagulan had had the unique distinction of leaving the firm in eight hours. He couldn't stand the haughty inspector who visited the camp that evening. The way he stood with one foot on the chair. And his words—"I have roughed it out under the white man. You too, should be ready to get a beating." And how his fellow supervisors vied with one another to start his dilapidated motor bike! Nagulan couldn't stand it. "To hell with you fools," he said and took the five o'clock bus.

Time tells who a fool is. The inspector had now bought a Yamaha 100. He had also laid the foundation for a new house. The supervisors too were well off.

There was a temple at the end of the slope. The bike seemed jubilant. If only the entire route sloped like this! The installments would be collected in no time.

He should now take the lane on the right, along the river bank. The shade had been courting the lane for a long time. The trees had witnessed the losing battle the sun had been waging here.

Between the trees and the river there were tall grass and cane shrubs. When the grass swayed in the breeze the boats in the river became visible. One evening he had brought his Yashica Electro 35 and taken a picture of the boats through the swaying reeds. When the film was developed, there were no boats in the picture!

A mile further, the trees started thinning. The gaps between the trees widened and then the trees simply vanished—like happiness abruptly ended.

And now a housing colony appeared.

Although he had been to Thangeswari's house many times, it was still difficult to locate it. The huts in the area were all alike. The one from which the sound of sewing machine came was Thangeswari's.

Nagulan leaned his bicycle on a coconut log and went inside. The odour of dried prawns filled the air. Thangeswari was cleaning fish. On seeing him she blushed.

"Just a minute," she walked to the well. Nagulan leaned against a coconut tree.

Nagulan had heard that the man who worked in a nearby jewellery shop spent the night at Thangeswari's. Whether or not he gave her money, he definitely should give her a bar of soap.

Whenever Thangeswari came to Nagulan's shop, she and the shop assistant Manoharan would crack bawdy jokes as if Nagulan never existed!

"The machine is giving trouble. Could you please come and see?"

"Top or bottom? If bottom, it needs oiling!"

They would go on along these lines.

Thangeswari brought the money. Nagulan wrote out a receipt for a hundred and twenty-five rupees.

"Never worry about our money. You need not come. We will ourselves call over to pay."

Nagulan got ready to leave. As if as an afterthought, Thangeswari said: "Could you please have a look at the machine? The thread gets stuck!"

Nagulan was stunned. An awkward moment. "Please! I have got another twenty-five customers to see. At this rate I cannot finish with them. I'll come tomorrow or I'll send my assistant."

Nagulan came to the threshold. He was probably the only person who had spent nine months in the Company without even knowing how to thread a needle. If not for the legalities involved he would have been happier to start a dispensary and spend his time with Disprin and Vicks vaporub.

Now, the scorching heat. Even the bicycle seemed to join him in the struggle. Darkness, sun, moonlight, rain. At times the bicycle seemed to come to life.

For the next stop, he had to pedal quite some distance. By the time he reached there it would be half past twelve.

However, he reached Krishnasamy's house earlier than he expected. Krishnasamy had just retuned from his paddy field. He usually discouraged Nagulan from visiting his house. Whenever he passed Nagulan's shop he would say, "Brother, don't trouble yourself. I will come here myself!" But that never happened.

Krishnasamy gave him a postdated cheque for five hundred rupees.

"Last time too, your cheque was returned. Don't know whether the company will accept this."

"No, no, there is money in my account. Why, even last time the problem was not credit. The second officer said that something was wrong with the signature!"

After issuing the receipt Nagulan came out. Another customer lived two houses away. There were special occasions—like the Pongal, Hindu New Year, the Deepavali, or the Festival season at the local temple—at which one could meet Gunaratnam. Gunaratnam was not just one case in point. It was very difficult to meet the men of the village. It was easier to meet them at Kannathiddy, Jaffna, or Sea Street, Colombo.

Each time he went to Gunaratnam's house, Nagulan's suspicion that they didn't need a machine was confirmed. There was no trace of any sewing going on there. In fact he had dusted the machine twice.

Mrs Gunaratnam moaned. "Brother, I haven't got the money order from him yet. As soon as I get it I'll call."

"Without fail?" Nagalan asked.

"Don't you trust me?"

"Alright," he said, disgusted, turning his bike.

He had to go five miles to look for the next account. He was tired.

As he pedalled, he thought, "Maybe no job is independent! Maybe nobody gets a job he likes!"

He, who threw up a job because he couldn't tolerate an inspector, was now a prisoner in another cell! Is the whole world made up of cells? Nagulan was ashamed of what he was doing just now, for the sake of a long line of masters from New York to Sri Lanka—masters whose faces he didn't know.

He could have given up this job too, but what could he have done after that? Darkness, with open jaws, was waiting to swallow him up. Could he go to Seeni's hardware store to while away the time writing bills? Or wear the headphones at Shanthi Studio and record cheap songs? What should he do?

Nagulan forgot that he was riding the bike. From here onwards it would be a stretch of paddy fields on both sides of the roads.

"Eight more days for the end of the month. Five miles shouldn't be a long distance," he consoled himself.

Translated by S Pathmanathan

Ahalya

S SIVASEGARAM

Stones.
Above the earth, beneath the earth,
hillocks and mountains,
rocks and fragments,
upright, fallen,
stones.

Her husband, the sage, was a stone.
The god was a liar, but
no stone he,
only a male deity who lived
to survive the curse.
And she who had lived like stone
coming alive for that instant alone
truly became a stone.

On a day much later,
a god who crossed the seas to rescue a lover
only to thrust her
into burning flames—
who feared the town's gossip
and exiled her—
a god, yet unworthy of touching a stone—
stumbled upon her.

Had she not changed again
stone becoming woman
to live like a stone with a stone,

Ahalya

Had she remained truly a stone
she might have stood forever,
a mountain peak, undestroyed by time.

Translated by Lakshmi Holmström

Glossary

Amman: Goddess; the consort of Lord Shiva
Anna: Older brother
Appa: Father
Appan: Father
Arichchuvadi: The Tamil alphabet
Cheetu: A way of pooling money
Chiththirai: The month of May
Dharshan: Admission to the presence of a god or saint
Ekel: The spine of a palm leaf
Enna: What?
Kachcheri: A central government office
Kadai: Shop
Kaiviyalam: A token sum of money given by an elder on New Year's day
Kamuku: An arecanut tree
Kandam: A major impediment caused by fate
Kanthor: Office
Karuththakolumban: A particularly tasty variety of mango
Kollivai devil: A ghost that looks like a flame
Kovil: Hindu Temple
Kudumi: Hair tied in a knot
Kumbam: Ceremonial vessel and coconut
Kurakkan Pittu: Food made out of a particular grain
Machchan: Cousin; used as a term of affection among friends
Madam: Dwelling place associated with religious organizations
Maruthu water: Medicinal water sprinkled on the head by Hindus before bathing on New Year's day
Matha Kovil: Church
Murugandy: A small village south of Jaffna, also known for its temple
Nallur: A city in Jaffna, known for its Murugan temple

Natchathiram: Star; zodiac sign
Ola: Palm leaf
Paadai: A structure on which a corpse is carried
Padalai: Gate
Pittu: Food made out of flour
Pongal: Sweet Rice; the ritual of cooking rice; harvest festival
Por: Literally "war". Also refers to coconuts used for breaking as a form of game.
Pottu: A dot placed on the forehead
Puvarasu: A common tree in the North of Sri Lanka
Rameswaram: A port city in South India
Salvai: A shawl that covers the upper part of the body, worn by men.
Santhanam: Sandalwood paste
Sulam: Trident, found in temples
Tali: A gold pendant given to the bride as a symbol of marriage
Thamby: Younger brother, also a term of polite address to someone younger
Thangachi: Younger sister, also a term of polite address to someone younger
Ther: Chariot
Thevaram: Religious song
Thinnai: An elevated space along the verandah of a house where people sit
Thiruvila: Temple festival
Thosai: A popular food shaped like a pancake
Thuravu: Renunciation
Ulundhu: Kind of lentils
Vairavar: One of the gods of the Hindu pantheon
Vetti: Cloth worn by men
Viputhi: Holy ash
Yal Devi: The morning train that runs between Colombo and Jaffna

Contributors

P Akilan received an MA in Art Criticism from the University of Baroda, India, and recently joined the University of Jaffna, Sri lanka, where he teaches fine arts. He belongs to the new generation of poets from Sri Lanka, his first collection of poems, *Pathunkukuli Naadkal,* having been published in 2001.

Ki Pi Aravindan is the pen name of Christopher Francis, who was born in 1953 in Jaffna, Sri Lanka. He moved to Paris as a refugee in 1991, after having been involved in the Tamil liberation struggle since 1970, and edited a quarterly literary magazine *Mounam* for several years. He started writing poetry in the late eighties and has published three collections of poems: *Ini Oru Vaikarai*(1991), *Mukam Kol* (1992) and *Kanavin Meethi* (1999). He also writes short stories.

B Balasooriyan is an Engineer by profession. He studied at the Technical University in Delft and lives in the Netherlands. He was one of the editors of the journal *Puthusu.*

Castro is young poet whose works have appeared in various literary magazines in Sri Lanka, India and in the UK.

R Cheran was born in 1960. He is the son of Mahakavi and hails from Alaveddy in Jaffna, Sri Lanka. He holds a doctoral degree in Sociology from York University, Canada and is currently a Research Associate at the Centre for Refugee Studies, York University. As a poet, journalist and academic, his activities have been motivated by his commitment to social justice. He has edited with others an important anthology of political poems entitled *Maranothul Valvom* (1985). His publications include *Irandavathu Suriya Uthayam* (1983), *Yaman*(1984), *Kaanal Vari* (1989), *Elumbuk Kuudukalin Urvalam* (1990), *Ini Thungathirukkum*

Neram (1994), and *Ni Ippozhluthu Irangum Aaru* (2000).

Ilangayarkone (real name N Sivagnanasundaram) is one of the three foremost writers of the modern Tamil short story in Sri Lanka. His first story appeared in *Kalaimagal* in Tamil Nadu, India, in 1930. His work also appeared in all the major periodicals of that time in Tamil Nadu, namely, *Sooraavali*, *Manikkodi*, *Baharathathaai*, *Sakthi*, and *Saraswathy*. His writings appeared in all the newspapers and magazines in Sri Lanka, and he wrote stage and radio plays, of which *London Kandiah,* broadcast over Radio Ceylon, was a major success. His short story "Vellipatha-saram" is considered one of the most significant to be written in Tamil in Sri Lanka. He served as an Officer in the Ceylon Administrative Service.

V I S Jayapalan, is a prolific poet from Neduntheevu, Sri Lanka, who now lives in Norway. He has been writing poems for over three decades. His first work *Suriyanodu Pesuthal* appeared in 1986. This was followed by several other signficant volumes including *Eelathu Mannum Enkal Mukangalum* (1986), *Namakkendru Oru Pulveli* (1987) and *Oru Akathiyin Paadal* (1991). He is at present actively involved in researching the caste structure prevailing among Tamils in Sri Lanka. He has also written short stories and two short novels.

Dominic Jeeva has been a writer for over fifty years. He has to his credit several publications of essays and collection of short stories, including *Paathukai* and *Saalaiyin Thiruppankal*. He won the Sahitya Award for Tamil short stories in 1961 for his collection entitled *Thanneeerum Kanneerum*. He is also the Editor of the literary journal *Mallikai*, which is in its 35th year of publication. In addition, he is a publisher who has brought out almost fifty books by other authors under his *Mallikai Pandal* programme.

A Jesurasa was born in Gurunagar, Jaffna, Sri Lanka. He has published a collection of short stories entitled *Tholaivum Iruppum Enaiya Kathaikalum* (1974) and a collection of poems called *Ariyappadaathavarkal Ninaivaaka*. He received the Sahitya Award for his short story collection in 1974. He also co-edited an important quarterly magazine called *Alai* (wave). His columns in *Thisai* (of which he was an associate editor) have been collected into a book entitled *Thoovaanam* (2001). He has also translated poems from other languages into Tamil and was co-editor of *Pathinoru Eelaththu Kavingnarkal,* an important collection of poetry.

Kasturi, or Vasanthy Ganeshan, was a poet and short-story writer who was born in 1968 in Urelu Chunnakam, Jaffna and died in 1991 while engaged in the Tamil liberation struggle. Her works, which are concerned with the oppression of the Tamil population by the State, were collected in a volume entitled *Kasthuriyin Aakkangal* (1992).

Mahakavi, orT Rudramoorthy, was born in Alaveddy, Jaffna, in 1927 and died in 1971. Starting in 1943, he wrote poetry under several pen names. One of the pioneers of modern Tamil poetry in Sri Lanka, Mahakavi introduced into it the rhythms of ordinary speech. He has written five epics *(kaaviynakal),* three stage plays in verse *(Paanaadakankal)* and ten radio plays. Best known as a playwright and poet, he was also co-editor of the first Tamil poetry journal in Ceylon called *Thenmoli.* Several of his works were published posthumously. His major works include: *Valli* (1955), *Kurumpa* (1966), *Kodai* (1970), *Veedum Veliyum* (1973) *Puthiyathoru Veedu* (1979) and *Mahakaviyin Aaru Kaaviyankal* (2000).

R Murugaiyan was born in 1935 at Kalvayal, a village in Chavakachcheri, Sri Lanka. An Arts and Science graduate, and later a member of the Sri Lanka Education Service, he was an editor in the Educational Publications Department of the Government of Sri Lanka and was responsible for creating the Tamil Scientific Vocabulary. He is considered one of the pioneers of modern Tamil literature in Sri Lanka, and is a poet, playwright, and critic. He is known for *Oru Varam* (1964), *Nedumpakal* (1967), *Kopuravasal* (1969), *Oru Silv Vithi Seyvom* (1972) and *Adhipahavan* (1978).

A Muttulingam, Appadurai Muttulingam, was born in Kokuvil, Sri Lanka. A Chartered Accountant by profession, his literary career started at the age of nineteen when he won the first prize in the all Ceylon Tamil short story competition conducted by *Thinakaran,* a national newspaper. His collected short story publications are: *Akka,* which included three prize winning stories; *Thikada Chakkaram,* which won the Lily Thevasikamani Award in India; *Vamsa Vruthi,* which won the Tamil Nadu Government first prize and the State Bank of India first prize; and *Vadakku Veethi,* which won the Sri Lanka Government Sahitya Academy award for the year 1998. His forthcoming collection of short stories is entitled "Maharajavin Railvandi."

K V Nadarajan was the editor of a fortnightly called *Vivasaayi,* a newspaper of the Northern Division Agricultural Producer's Co-operative in Jaffna. He wrote a collection of short stories entitled *Yaalapaanak Kathaikal.*

Neelaavanan, or K Sinadurai (1931–1975), was born in Periya Neelaavanai in the Eastern Province of Sri Lanka. He has written under several pseudonyms. He is the author of two poetry epics *(kaaviyankal),* plays in verse *(Paanaadakankal)* and short stories that appeared in *Uruvakak Kathaikal* and *Nadaichchiththirankal.* He was the editor of a short-lived literary magazine titled Paadummeen. A posthumous collection called *Vali* came out in 1976. *Nilaavanan Kathaigal* was published in 2001.

M A Nuhman was born in 1944 in Kalmunai in the Eastern province. Currently a professor in the department of Tamil at the University of Peradeniya, he has published extensively during the last two decades. His poetry collections include *Thathamarum Perarkalum* (1977), *Azhiya Nizhalkal* (1982), and *Mazhai Natkal Varum* (1983). He has published a book of translations titled *Palesthina Kavithaigal* (2000) and three works of literary criticism, *Thiranivu Katturaigal* (1985) *Marxiyamum Ilakiya Thiranaivum* (1987), and *Bharathiyin Mozhi Chinthanaigal* (1999).

Oorvashi, or Jhuvaneswari Arutpragasam, was born in Jaffna in 1956. She holds a degree from the University of Jaffna in Mathematics and Science and is currently a lecturer in the College of Education in Batticaloa. Her poetry has been included in a number of significant anthologies.

M Ponnambalam was born in Pungudutivu, one of the islands off

Jaffna, in Sri Lanka in 1939. His first collection of poems *Athu* was published in 1968 in Madras. *Kaali Leelai* is a comprehensive collection of his poems Among his critical works, *Yatharthamum Athmarthamum* (1991) is a notable achievement. *Kadalum Karaiyum* is his short story collection. He now lives in Colombo. Ponnampalam is a brother of Mu Thalayasingam, an outstanding writer, literary critic and a social reformist who died at the early of age of thirty-five.

S Ponnuthurai, popularly known as Espo, was born in Nallur, Jaffna in 1932. A major short-story writer known for his innovations in plot, style and technique, he has also written novels, plays, poems and critical articles. *Thee, Sadanku, Vee, Nanavidaithoythal, Avaa* and *Ini* are among his publications. During the last several years he has become a publisher and has brought out approximately forty books through Mithra Publications, Chennai, India. He now lives in Australia.

N K Ragunathan has published stories in *Eelakesari, Ponni, Suthanthiran, Thinakaran, Virakesari* and *Thinakkural* in Sri Lanka and in *Saraswathi* and *Thamarai* in Tamil Nadu. He is one of the pioneers of the Progressive Writers in Sri Lanka. His first collection, titled Nilavile Pesuvom, appeared in 1962, and his second collection, *Thasamankalam,* was published in 1996. Among his works, *Kandan Karunai,* a play based on the traditions of folk theatre received considerable praise and was performed very successfully.

N S M Ramiah is an important writer from the hill country; he was born in Badulla in 1931. He first wrote radio plays, which were broadcast over Radio Ceylon. His collection of short stories, *Oru Koodai Kolunthu,* was published in 1980 and it received the Sahitya award in that year.

Ranjakumar was born in Karaveddy, Jaffna in 1961. A printer by profession, he started writing short stories in the mid 80s. He also writes literary reviews. *Mohavasal* is his first collection of short stories.

A M Rashmy was born in Akkaraipattu in the Eastern Province. He is a well-known painter who has contributed as an illustrator for the news-

Contributors

paper *Sarinihar* and *Moonravathu Manithan*, a literary magazine in Colombo. A young writer of promise, his collection of poems entitled *Kavu Kollappatta Valvu* will be published in January 2002.

K Saddanathan was born in Velanai, Jaffna and began writing short stories in the 70s. His collections are called *Maatram* (1980), *Ulaa* (1992) and *Saddanathan Kathaigal* (1995). The latter received the Sahitya award.

A Santhan was born in Suthumalai, Jaffna. He has written short novels and very short stories. His books include *Mulaikal, Oru Pidi Man,* and *Oddumaa.* A surveyor by profession, he has travelled widely and his important travelogue (based on his travels in the former Soviet Union) is titled *Oli Cirantha Nattil.* He also writes in English, in which his most recent publication is *In Their Own Worlds* (2000).

S Selvi, Selvanithi Thiyagarajah, was born in 1960. A feminist writer who studied drama and theatre at the University of Jaffna, her poems have appeared in several anthologies. A collection titled *Selvi Sivaramani Kathaigal*, which also included Sivaramani's poetry, appeared in Tamil Nadu. She is a recepient of a PEN Award. She died in 1991.

S Sivalingam was born in 1940 in Pandiruppu in the Eastern Province. He graduated from Kerala with a degree in Science and served as a teacher and a principal. A major poet and short story writer, he also wrote two novels. *Neervalaiyangal* (1988) brings together some of his major poems. His collection of short stories will be published in the near future.

S Sivaramani died in 1991, when she had become known for her political and feminist poems. She graduated from the University of Jaffna, having read Drama and English. She was one of the founder members of the Women's Study Circle in Jaffna. The collection entitled *Sivaramani Kavithaigal*, which was published in Canada, Sri Lanka and India, brings together her poetry.

S Sivasegaram was born in 1942 in Inuvil, Jaffna. Currently, he is professor of Mechanical Engineering, University of Peradeniya. A poet, critic, essayist and translator, he has produced many volumes of poetry including *Nathikarai Mungil* (1983), *Ceppanitta Padimangal* (1987), *Thevi Ezhunthaal* (1989), *Eekalaiva Puumi* (1993) *Porin Muhangal* (1996), and *Vadali* (1999). His collected essays are titled *Marapum Maarksiyamum* (1987), *Thamizhum Ayalum* (1992), and *Thamizhil Tharippuk Kurikalin Payanapaadu* (1994). His translations have also appeared in three volumes.

Solaikkili, or A M Atheek, was born in Kalmunai in the Eastern Province in 1957. He started writing poetry in the 80s and established himself as a major poet. *Nanum Oru Punai, Ettavathu Naragam* and *Kaakam Kalaitha Kanavu Aaniver Aruntha Naan, Paambu Narambuu Manithan,* and *Paniyil Mozhi Ezhuthi* are among his major publications. His collected works will appear in January 2002.

Thamaraichchelvi is a short-story writer and novelist who works as a teacher in Vanni, in the Northern Province. In 1993 her novel entitled *Thakam* won an award for the best novel of the year. She has also published two collections of short stories.

Uma Varatharajan was born in 1956 in Kalmunai in the Eastern Province. His works have appeared in both Sri Lanka and India. *"Arasanin Varukai,"* which appeared in *India Today,* won widespread acclaim. He has also edited a literary magazine called *Kala Ratham* and writes reviews on literature and the arts. He is an important columnist for several literary magazines. Ulmana Yaathirai is his collection of short stories.

S Vilvaratnam was born in 1950 in Punkudutheevu in the Northern province and began writing in 1970. He emerged as a major writer in the early eighties. Akangalum Mukangalum, Kaatruveli Kiramam and *Kaalathuyar* are his best known collections of poetry. *Netriman* came out in 2000. His complete collection of poems entitled *Uyirthelum Kaalaththirkkakka* was published in 2001. He now lives in Trincomalee.

Translators

Suresh Canagarajah is a graduate from Peradeniya University and received his doctorate from the United States. He is currently Associate Professor of English at the State University of New York. He has published widely in literature and linguistics.

A J Canagaratna graduated from the University of Ceylon, Peradeniya and started his career as a journalist with the Lakehouse Group of Papers. He has translated Sri Lankan Tamil writing into English since the 1950s. His essays and translations cover a broad range of topics including literature, film, economics, the environment and medicine. He retired recently from the University of Jaffna where he taught in the department of English. His published works include *Maththu, Senkaavalar Thalaivar Jesunathar* (2000) and a selection of translations titled Marximum Ilakkiyamum. Maththu was awarded the Sahitya Award in 1970.

Lakshmi Holmström studied at Madras and Oxford Universities, and is currently a freelance writer and translator. Her critical articles and reviews have appeared in various journals in India, Europe and the United States. She has translated a number of important Tamil novels and short stories, by Mouni, Puthumaipithan, Sundara Ramasamy, Ambai, Ashokamitran, Na Muthusamy, Bama and Imayam. Her retelling of the two Tamil epics *Silappadikaram* and *Manimekalai* was published by Orient Longman. She lives in Norwich, England, where she was a teacher of English for many years.

Chelva Kanaganayakam graduated with a degree in English from Sri Lanka and taught English literature at the University of Jaffna from 1976-1981. He currently teaches English at the University of Toronto, Canada. His most recent book, *Counterrealism and the Indian Novel*, will be published in March 2002.

S Pathmanathan earned his degree from the University of Jaffna, and then became a lecturer in English at the Palaly Training College. Apart from being a translator, he is also an accomplished poet in Tamil. His collection of poems, *Vadakkiruthal,* was published in 1998. A collection of Tamil translations of African Short Stories was published in October 2001.

S Rajasingham taught in Nigeria before becoming a lecturer in English at the Technical College in Jaffna. He has actively promoted English studies in Jaffna and has translated poetry and fiction from Tamil to English.

S Thirunavukarasu is an Engineer by profession, having attended universities in Sri Lanka and in England. The brother of the well-known writer S Sivagnanasunderam (Nandhi), he has been, for the last three decades, actively involved in the arts. Theatre and film are among his major interests. In 2001 he published a book entitled *Stepping Into Success.* He now lives in Canada.

Acknowledgements

A project such as this one entails the daunting task of bringing together authors and translators who live in various parts of the world. Without the assistance of many, even a modest anthology could not have been put together. Many thanks to Professor A Shanmugadas, Dr S Sivalingarajah and Mr M Ragunathan for their help in locating material and for their suggestions; to Dr R Cheran and Mr M Nithiyanandan for their valuable feedback; to Mrs Sivagurunathan and Mrs Maheswary Balasundaram for their careful typing and word processing. I am indebted to M G Vassanji and Nurjehan Aziz whose rigorous editorial skills and enthusiasm have helped immensely in shaping the book. Some of the material has appeared in the *Toronto South Asian Review* and the *Journal of South Asian Literature*.